Spinning Out of Control

Kit Barrie

Contents

Content Warning

THIS STORY DEALS WITH the aftermath of a severe car crash in which the main human character, Caleb, was badly injured on one side of his body, including the amputation of his dominant hand and severe facial scarring from burns. Throughout the narrative, Caleb deals with post-traumatic stress disorder (PTSD,) depression, chronic pain, and suicidal ideations.

The main monster character, Teracht, deals with mild Obsessive Compulsive Disorder (OCD), anxiety, and agoraphobia (fear of leaving the house.) There is discussion of his life in the monster world that included cannibalism and non-consensual mating between his species; neither of those occur on page or to the main character.

This story contains explicit, consensual sexual situations between adults and is not meant for children.

Chapter 1

Caleb

It had been seven months. Seven fucking months since my life came to a crashing halt. Just long enough for everyone to forget or stop offering help, and just long enough for the most obvious issues to be treated with surgery and physical therapy. They said, "Life goes on," and it sure fucking did, even with me barely holding onto the reins.

I was lucky to be alive. Everyone said so. Seeing pictures of my car afterwards, they were right. If the driver of the other car had struck my driver side instead of my passenger side, I probably wouldn't have even known what hit me; it just would have been lights out. I couldn't even be angry at the guy who hit me. It was his fault for running the red light, and he died. I didn't. Which meant that I was the only one living with the result of his fuck up. His family was sorry for what happened, to him and to me, but words didn't change what the accident did or what it took from me.

I didn't remember much about it, which was probably a blessing in disguise, considering the damage. I didn't know that third degree burns don't necessarily hurt right away, but I found out they hurt like a bitch when my wounds started to heal. I also didn't realize that my hand was gone until I woke up two days later in the hospital. You would think that you'd know when you are suddenly minus one significant body part, but I didn't. Not until I tried to touch my bandaged face and found nothing at the end of my right forearm.

But the hands on the clock still turned, even though I felt like time had stopped for me. I had surgeries to fix the broken bones and torn muscles in my right side and shoulder. I had physical therapy to keep the skin on my burned face, neck, and arm from tightening too much. I had occupational therapy to learn how to use my left hand for everything my right had once done. And now, I was on my own. Plopped back into the unforgiving world like a baby bird that only just learned to fly.

The first blow when I rejoined the real world was not unexpected. My modeling agency dropped me. I went from one of the most requested photo shoot models in the state to being jobless. I couldn't blame them; I would have done the same thing. I couldn't even stand to look at myself in the mirror. Why would anyone else want to pay me to take photographs with my ruined face, uneven features, and missing hand?

The insurance payout would at least keep my bills paid for a while. I had never considered that there could be a price on what my body was worth, but apparently there was. But now what? My life had changed in literally seconds, and I was supposed to just adapt to this new "normal." Life continued on around me, as if my whole world hadn't stopped that afternoon in August in that intersection.

I tried to get back to my life as best I could. And then I discovered how much people suck. Or, at least, the people I knew. The few who were willing to hang out with me at all acted like I was dying. Hushed voices, not asking me any questions about how I was feeling, making small talk like we were strangers, giving vague promises to hang out again soon or to let them know if I needed anything. After those few pulled away and didn't reach out anymore, I was okay with that. I would rather be alone than with people who I thought were my friends but couldn't face the tragedy that I had to live with every day.

But the problem was, I didn't want to be alone. I appreciated me-time like anyone else, and I was really glad I did not have a roommate in my one-bedroom apartment as I tried to adapt to life without my dominant hand. But I had always been social. I liked going to parties and clubs, hanging out at the bar with my so-called friends, catching a movie, or even just getting together and playing video games. I had no siblings, and I wasn't seeing anyone seriously. I was actually sort of glad I hadn't been dating anyone when it happened, because, even though it would have been nice to have someone there, if that person had decided they couldn't handle being with me, with my burned face and missing appendage, I don't know what I would have done. My parents lived out of state, though my mom came to stay with me when I first got out of the hospital. She tried multiple times to convince me to move back in with them, but I refused. While I knew she meant well, I could still take care of myself. I didn't want or need to be treated like a kid, even if things were more difficult now.

I tried going to the meetings for people recovering from trauma. I tried talking to the therapist assigned to me. I tried talking to people online. None of it helped. If I'm being honest, a lot of it made it worse, and my own attitude wasn't helping either. My anger and frustration kept growing until I felt like it would drown me. There was no up-side to this. No silver lining, no lesson I was supposed to learn, no moment of clarity or realization.

The only thing that even remotely helped were the antidepressants. It took several months for my doctor and I to get a medication and dosage that actually helped me. I had never been someone who thought they would be dependent on medication to be able to function. "There's no shame in taking what your body needs," my doctor had said. I knew that was true, but it was another mentality shift I had to adjust to in a very short amount of time while my world was on fire around me.

I used to think I was a confident guy, maybe even a little cocky at times, though what 29-year-old isn't? I was handsome, I had a job I loved, and my life was good. And then that all ended.

The very first time I went out in public on my own after my accident without bandages and dressings on my face, a little boy on the sidewalk had burst into screams and told his mother, "You said the monsters didn't live over here!"

His mother had tried to hush him and cast me an embarrassed, apologetic look as she pulled her kid away, but the damage was done. I was not human anymore. At least, not where people could see me. I had barely looked in a mirror since I had returned to my apartment from my long stint in the hospital, but after that, I took down every single mirror in my house and hid them in the back of my closet. I had things delivered, and if I left my apartment, even to just get the mail or take out the trash, I put on a facemask or a scarf. It often hurt, like I was being stabbed over and over again, the pinched skin and healing nerves so painfully sensitive that I wanted to curl up into a ball and die instead of dealing with it. Even the sheets on my bed or the gentlest fall of water from my shower could cause insane amounts of pain that my prescribed medications wouldn't even begin to touch. I don't know what hurt worse though, the physical pain or the emotional pain. And feeling that sort of constant misery all the time was exhausting, in every sense of the word.

It's hard to pull yourself out of that sort of darkness when you're so fucking exhausted just from being alive.

That was when I heard about the Monster Match app. I had known about monsters in our world for a while now, even encountered a few here and there in my various modeling gigs. It was kind of scary to realize that monsters not only existed but were in the very place I lived in. I lived in Edgewind, which was one of the towns that had been turned into a safe haven for monsters to integrate themselves into human society. But they tended to stick together in specific areas, and while some of them did venture beyond that, I did not encounter them with any sort of regularity in my day-to-day life, especially after I holed up in my apartment like the apocalypse had come.

But as the weeks alone turned into months, with nothing in my life changing except whether or not I felt like getting out of bed each day, I joined the Monster Match app and started to browse it, more out of sheer morbid curiosity than anything. I knew so little about monsters, and reading their profiles gave me a better idea of the many types of creatures that had come into our world. Their abilities and looks varied so much. Some of them were smaller, even smaller than humans, and some were much bigger. Looking at their pictures was more interesting to me though. Some very obviously were not human, with multiple eyes, sharp teeth, grotesque features, wings, or fur. But others could pass for human with a few special articles of clothing or some basic makeup tricks and contacts. That made me wonder two things. First, if I had ever met a monster that I hadn't realized was a monster because of how well they hid it. And second, if I myself could actually pass as a monster rather than human.

That thought made my insides tighten. I was not born a monster. I was even blessed with good looks. I had been a moderately good student through high school, popular, had lots of friends. I went to community college for a few years but did not have a major in mind. Then I was offered a modeling contract by a recruiter, my career took off, and I had almost ten years of life being pretty damn good. And now what? I was not yet 30; I still had probably another forty or fifty years left in me. That was also a sobering thought, that I would probably live longer without my dominant hand than I had with it. This was who I was now, like it or not.

It was March when I was browsing the Monster Match app again. I had had several monsters try to match with me, and more than a few monster dicks and maybe-not-dicks sent to me in messages too. I still had not replied to any of them. I was sure a lot of them just saw my profile picture, one of my old photos from early last year before my life changed so dramatically, and decided I was hot. But today, a new profile popped up that I had not seen before. It was a basic one, with less detail than the premium memberships had. The face in the little box on the screen was obviously a selfie. The creature's skin was dark gray, with a shock of almost white hair that seemed to be standing straight up from its head. From what I could see, it didn't seem to have clothes on, though its skin looked to be almost like molded plastic or some kind of armor, in segments over its chest and arms. The creature was giving the camera the barest hint of a smile, the sort of look you had when you weren't really sure if you were worthy of a photo. But what caught my attention were the eyes, eight in all, that peered into the camera, black as night.

I scanned the new monster's profile curiously. The name was listed as "Teracht," and the pronouns were listed as "he/him." His species was listed as "Atauri," but my internet search of that turned up nothing that told me what that was. He listed his occupation as "spinner," though I doubted he meant he led a spin class at a gym. His bio blurb was pretty straight-forward. He was not new to the human world, but he said that he very rarely left his house and would like any potential partner to come to his place. I wondered if he realized that made him sound like a serial killer. He mentioned he was a little shy as well. That was interesting. If the monsters I had met before and the number of PMs with dicks in them were any indication, most monsters were pretty outgoing.

Something inside me tightened as I scanned his

information again. If he didn't leave his house, which seemed a little odd, it wasn't like he probably had that much company. I wondered if he had any human friends at all or if he even knew any humans? And if he did, would he care what they looked like? His profile listed him as seeking romance or friendship. I had never done more than browse the app, but the longer I looked at the sweet, hopeful smile Teracht was giving the camera, the more I found myself wondering if maybe this monster would be open to me venturing ever so slowly back into society. I swallowed hard, and, before I could talk myself out of it, I hit the button to match with him.

Chapter 2

Teracht

I DID NOT RESPOND to the match on the Monster Match app for several days, only looked at the profile. Caleb only had the left half of his face visible to the camera, his golden blond hair obscuring part of his right side, but what I could see was exquisite. He had mentioned that he was a former model in his profile, and I could see it. With his shiny hair and sea-blue eyes, he looked like the sort of man who would work at a beach or be a movie star. I already knew that if he was on TV or in a movie, I would watch it every day. Why was someone so gorgeous seeking a partner on a monster dating app? Surely, he could have his pick of any number of human partners.

I had only been on the app for a few days. My friend, Cael, had come by with questions for me regarding the man he had met on the dating app that he was having feelings for. When he left, he had encouraged me to finally put myself on the app too. I was happy for him. Cael was a good monster. Lonely, like me, and we got along well enough, considering our eccentricities. He did not have a home, just living and existing where he pleased. And his voice could make humans fall unconscious when they heard him for the first time. I had not, which surprised both of us when we first met, though he usually remained invisible when he came for a visit. With my larger range of vision and multiple eyes, his eldritch form made me feel like static was tingling under my skin when I looked at him. I had thought that might make him unhappy and not want to continue our relationship, but he was a surprisingly kind and astute monster. He stopped by at least once a week to see me, which I very much appreciated. In the time I had been in the human world, I had only ever left my house to go to the military base when requested, usually for their naturalization classes, like where I had met Cael. Otherwise, I stayed in my home.

I had been a little concerned when I first arrived in the human world, knowing that in order to stay, I would have to have a job. I would have done anything asked of me to ensure I was allowed to remain. The military examined my spider webs, and whatever they discovered, they were delighted and intrigued by it. They asked if I could provide more for them, and I had tried very hard not to laugh. I was a spider, after all. Spinning was natural to me, and I would do it anyway for my own comfort. So, I agreed to provide them with multiple kinds of webbing, with various tensile strengths and stickiness. And, to my delight, they said I could do that from the home I was given, if I was more comfortable that way. I had a feeling my webs were much more valuable than they were letting on, so they were willing to make concessions to get it, but I was perfectly fine with that arrangement. I could be alone, safe, away from prying eyes and predators, doing what I knew how to do. I could even experiment with my abilities, something I hadn't been able to do in the monster world, where spinning was the way that I survived.

When I discovered that I could watch human television in my home while I did my web work, I was over the moon, as the humans said. Humans had such expressive forms of art, and television had such a variety of stories and styles. I could use it to learn human language, culture, mannerisms, societal structure, and any other number of things. Between spinning as much as I could to make myself useful, and the fact that I only needed an hour or two of sleep a day to feel rested, I spent those first months in the human world watching a probably unhealthy amount of media.

I didn't regret it. I was actually enjoying this new life I had created for myself. If I had remained in the monster world, I very likely would have been dead by now. I was a gargantuan spider by human standards, but not by monster standards. I was downright puny compared to even the smaller males of my species. The likeliness that I would be able to successfully breed and escape with my life was zero, if I was not cannibalized by others of my kind first. In our land, only the strongest survived, and that was not me. There were no familial ties to bond us together either. I had to make my own way. So, when I heard that there were portals to another world that was letting monsters come in, I jumped at the chance.

And now I was too afraid to respond to an attractive human on a dating app.

I wanted to. Maybe it had been a mistake listing that I was interested in both friendship and romance. How did I know what this guy was looking for? I might have already messed things up for us, and I hadn't even responded to him yet. So, I waited until Cael came for his next visit.

"Cael, you got me into this, now I need you to tell me what to do," I told him when he arrived at my house, slipping unseen inside, but my senses immediately knew where he was. I held out my phone to him, Caleb's profile already on the screen, as it had been for the last four hours just today.

"He matched with you," Cael said, as if I hadn't realized the obvious.

"I know that," I said with a sigh. "But I don't know what to say to him."

"Ask him about things he likes," Cael suggested. He seemed to look closer at the profile, and I felt his smile, the strange vibrations of it going through me like a handshake.

"You watch enough movies to know what things humans like to do."

"But you watch actual humans," I said, feeling like this was the same conversation we had had last week but in reverse.

"*Caleb* seems nice," Cael said, and I rolled all eight of my eyes.

"You're saying that because his name is similar to yours," I said, not actually joking.

"His last name is Webster?" Cael asked with a laugh that probably would have a human unconscious on the floor but did nothing more than annoy me. "That is perfect, Teracht, maybe even meant to be."

"Can you be serious, please?" I asked. "I don't want to mess this up."

Cael was instantly back to his usual sincere self. "Just be honest with him," he said. "Tell him you haven't done this before, and you're nervous but want to make a good impression on him."

"What if he doesn't like me?"

I felt Cael shrug. "All you can do is be yourself. If he doesn't like that, then he isn't worth your time."

I sighed again. "He's the first human that's matched with me. Is that too soon to think about anything beyond friendship?"

And then I could have kicked myself. Cael had struggled to find someone to connect with on the Monster Match app.

I think he only was able to find his current human after a lot of trouble, and yet I had a gorgeous human who had messaged me within days of joining the site.

"Just see where it goes," Cael said, not seeming affronted by my good fortune in relationship-hunting. "It might not work out, but cross that bridge if you get to it."

"Okay. Thank you, Cael, I appreciate it," I said, giving him a tentative smile. "I'll message him back tonight."

Chapter 3

Caleb

I HAD BUTTERFLIES IN my stomach as I walked through the "monster" area of Edgewind. Some of the creatures passing me looked humanoid, others did not. I wasn't the only human in this area, at least. Most of them did not spare me a glance, which I was grateful for with my scarf wrapped securely around my face and my winter hat pulled down over my head. With the cold weather, at least I could get away with hiding my scars beneath a scarf.

It had been several days before I had heard back from Teracht on the Monster Match app. I had assumed he had not been interested when I didn't hear back within the first day or two. But he finally did message me. His very first message was an apology that he took so long to contact me, but he was new to relationships and had been nervous.

That was kind of endearing, a monster being nervous about contacting a human. We had only exchanged a few messages back and forth, but I had already agreed to come over to his house that Saturday afternoon.

I wondered about the wisdom of that choice as I took the bus the short distance across town to Teracht's area. But what worried me even more about it was the realization that I didn't actually care. I hadn't told anyone where I was going either, not having anyone I was still friends with that I felt comfortable telling about my monster meeting. If something went sideways and this monster was actually a serial killer or something else, no one would know or care where I had disappeared to. And that was strangely okay with me. I knew that was probably just the loneliness and PTSD talking, but nothing was pulling me out of the spiral I had pushed myself into. I debated being that asshole and just cancelling the whole encounter, but the thought of going back to my empty apartment to once again be alone with nothing but my thoughts felt like it might crush me like a bug. So, I forced myself to walk the block and a half from the bus stop to Teracht's house.

I double checked the address on my phone. It was a simple two-story house with a white picket fence that didn't stand out in any way from those around it except that the curtains over the window were a little more lacy-looking than I usually saw. I opened the gate and crossed the short distance from the sidewalk to the step leading to the front door. My jaw clenched a bit. I could still turn around and walk away. I wasn't sure if that would be more painful than potential rejection once Teracht saw my face.

Fuck it, I thought grimly. *If a monster judges you too, then you'll know it's worth giving up.* I pressed the doorbell with my thumb, hearing it chime inside. There was a slight pause, and I took a few deep breaths before the lock clicked and the door swung open.

I was not sure what I had been expecting beyond the basics of Teracht's picture. I was expecting the dark skin and black eyes. He had mentioned in our short text exchange that he was a sort of spider-looking creature, but actually seeing him in person, slightly larger than me, was something else.

Teracht had dark gray skin that had a slight sheen to it, like the wings of a beetle. His hair was a lighter shade of gray, almost white, and stood straight up from his head like an anime character; the strands were silky, almost like thick webbing. I wondered if it naturally stayed like that or if he used an insane amount of product to keep it that way. His body was segmented in a way that reminded me of a centaur, with a human torso leading down to a round, furry abdomen, followed by a bulbous hind part that seemed much too big for the rest of his body. He had eight spider-like legs that were attached to the middle part of him, in addition to two arms on his torso that were fairly human-like except that his pointed fingers were more visibly segmented, like a robot or an anatomical doll. His eyes were bright black. Two of them were set on either side of his nose like a human's, but then he had six smaller ones scattered across his forehead. They were like onyx gemstones stuck into his flawless skin. And all of them were focused on me.

"Caleb?" he asked. His voice was soft and sweet, a little airy too, and he hit the hard 'C' of my name with just a bit of a hissing sound.

I swallowed and nodded. "Yeah."

He smiled slightly and held out his humanoid right hand toward me to shake. "I'm Teracht."

I was glad he pronounced that first so I didn't have to guess on it, but then I realized my first dilemma. I extended my left hand, taking his right awkwardly and giving it a slight shake. He looked a little confused but then gave me another shy smile. He had beautiful lips, I noticed.

"Please, come in." He gestured aside and stepped back so I could enter. "You can leave your boots on if you like, I'm not on the floor that often."

I had to roll that around in my head for a minute until I stepped inside and made the connection. His house was two stories but was very open, with tall, vaulted ceilings. And there were spider webs everywhere. Along the walls, strung across the ceiling, attached to the stair banister. My mind immediately went to several movies with giant monster spider lairs full of webs. I half-expected to see human-shaped cocoons hanging from the ceiling, and I was relieved that there were not.

"May I take your coat?" Teracht asked. His words sounded uncertain, like he wasn't sure if he was supposed to say them out loud.

I turned to him, swallowing hard. Taking off my coat would reveal my missing hand, and undoing my scarf would reveal my face. I couldn't stay wrapped up in my protective coverings forever. If he was going to be upset with me and thinking I was kittenfishing him, better to get it over with now before we had done more than say hello. "Hey, um, before that..." He looked at me curiously, and I swallowed again. "There's something I have to tell you."

Teracht gazed back at me. I didn't think it was possible for eight eyes to look confused, but all of them did. "Yes?" he asked.

"I, um, was in an accident," I said slowly.

Teracht immediately looked concerned. "Are you all right?"

"No, it... not on my way here," I said quickly, and he looked relieved. "Months ago. And the picture of me on the app is from... before that."

Teracht continued to gaze back at me, and I realized he was waiting for me to explain. I hesitated before slowly reaching up to undo my scarf, letting it slip down around my shoulders to reveal my scarred face and neck.

Teracht's many eyes were still unblinking. I couldn't tell what he was thinking with that deep stare. I slowly pulled my right arm from my jacket pocket, letting the empty cuff hang down. I watched the connection form in his mind before he lifted his eyes to meet mine again. "Does it hurt?"

I wasn't sure what I had been expecting him to ask, but that wasn't it. I exhaled sharply, my left hand automatically flying up to touch the puckered skin at my jawline. "Um... a little?"

"I'm sorry," Teracht said. His voice was hesitant. I waited for him to say something else, maybe to tell me that I should go, or thanks but no thanks, or that I looked nothing like the image on my profile. But he only gazed back at me, his head tipping slightly as if studying me, all eight eyes unblinking.

I shifted a little under his gaze. Why had I ever thought this might be a good idea? "Sorry. I can go," I said, reaching for my scarf to pull it back up.

"Oh. Do you want to?" His voice was so quiet, I could barely hear him.

I blinked. "Uh..."

His most human-placed eyes lowered to the ground, though the other six continued to gaze at me, and that felt very weird. "Am I not what you expected?"

"I... what?" How in the world had he interpreted my offering to leave as *him* being the one at fault?

Teracht looked up at me again, though his head stayed ducked a little. He might have been looking at me through his eyelashes, if he had any. "Did I do something wrong?"

"No!" I said quickly, both of my arms coming up as if to stop his words. "No, you're just fine." I had really not given him much thought since I walked in, too focused on what he would think of me. "I meant… if my face… bothers you?"

Teracht blinked all of his eyes. "Your face doesn't bother me."

"Oh." I felt heat rush to my cheeks. "Um…"

We stared at each other for what felt like an uncomfortably long time before I slowly said, "Okay. Sorry, I totally made this awkward."

Teracht just stared at me for another moment, looking uncertain. Every moment of silence felt like a needle in my back, so I took off my coat and scarf, holding it out to him where he still stood between me and the door.

At the proffered coat, Teracht seemed to shake himself out of whatever had caused his silence. He took my jacket and hung it up in a little closet by the door. "Would you like to sit?" he asked, gesturing to one of the only pieces of furniture in the entire room. It was a cream-colored couch, made with some sort of soft fabric, and there was not a single mark on it. No dents in the cushions, no crumbs or hair on the fibers. "It's new," he said, as if reading my mind. "I do not have a lot of furniture."

"You got a couch specifically for me?" I asked in surprise.

Teracht's cheeks colored a little. "Yes," he said.

I wasn't sure how to feel about that, suddenly feeling like an inconvenience if the spider creature had bought new furniture just because he was having someone come over. I gingerly sat down on the edge of the couch as if I would break it. Teracht watched me closely. I gave him a small, forced smile. "It's nice."

He looked relieved at my comment. "I'm glad."

"Why don't you have furniture?" I asked, glancing around the open floor space.

Teracht's cheeks were still dark as he replied, "I sit on my web, so I have no need for it."

"Oh." Of course, that made sense, I supposed. His web was so dense in the open space and came down so far in some places that I would have to duck my head to not catch my hair in it.

"May I offer you something to drink?" Teracht asked, and the formality of his words made me smile just a bit.

"I'm good, thanks," I said, and he nodded. I watched curiously as he moved with much more grace than I would expect from someone with a body shape like his, his spider legs seeming to attach to the web that barely moved under what was likely his not insubstantial weight. He walked as easily along the webbing as I might have on a hardwood floor, before he settled onto a large patch of it just a little to my left, sitting down and folding his legs under him, almost like a cat.

I cleared my throat, suddenly feeling extremely self-conscious. It had been a long time since I had actually been on a date, and the last few times, it had been with a human, and usually at a bar or restaurant, or at least somewhere with more people. Now, it was just me and the giant spider gazing curiously down at me. "So, uh… how long have you been in the human world?"

"Oh." Teracht seemed surprised by the question. "Just about a year."

"Are you liking it?" I asked.

Teracht nodded. "I am. What I have seen so far, anyway. I rarely go out."

"Yeah, you mentioned that in your profile," I said. "So, what do you do then?"

"I have anything I need delivered," Teracht said. "And my webbing is picked up by courier each day."

Ah, 'spinner' made sense now. "What is your web used for?"

Teracht shrugged. "I honestly have no idea. The military seemed interested in it when I came here. And it's something I can do from home."

"Why don't you go out?" I asked, though the words felt hypocritical in my mouth.

Teracht's cheeks colored a little, and his gaze dropped. "I… I just…"

Obviously, I had hit a nerve there. I waved my hand. "You don't have to answer, it's your business anyway."

Teracht nodded and went silent, gazing back at me. The weight of all eight of those eyes on me suddenly felt like an elephant standing on my chest. Why had I thought that meeting with a creature with so many eyes, when all I wanted was to disappear, was a good idea?

"Look, um... I'm sure you want to know what happened," I said, gesturing with my left hand to my missing right one and my scarred cheek.

Teracht blinked his eight eyes in unison. "Only if you wish to tell me."

"It was a car accident, back in August. Some guy ran the light and hit my car. I got pretty banged up."

"I can see that." I couldn't tell if Teracht was saying that with sincerity or not.

"If it bothers you, I can go," I said, swallowing hard.

"Why would it bother me?" Teracht asked in confusion, cocking his head slightly. His hair stayed perfectly in place, and I wondered if it did just naturally grow like that.

"Cause I don't look like I did in my picture."

Teracht stared at me. "Yes, you do."

I frowned. "It's one of my old pictures. From before my accident."

Teracht didn't respond, just gazing back at me, as if waiting for me to continue. I cleared my throat, suddenly wishing now that I had taken him up on that drink. "I guess I just... didn't want to show my face on camera."

"Why not?" Teracht asked.

I narrowed my eyes a little. "Why would I?"

"Aren't you a model?" Teracht asked in confusion.

"I was. Before my accident."

"But not anymore?"

Anger surged briefly in my chest. Was he trying to be

funny? "No. Not since the accident."

Teracht frowned a little. "Why did you stop?"

I raised a brow. "They fired me."

"Why?" Teracht asked in surprise.

I stared at him. "Uh, it's pretty obvious." I gestured to my face.

Teracht still looked confused. "Is it?"

I glared at him. "It's the first fucking thing that people notice, so yeah, I'd say it's pretty obvious."

"But it's your face."

"Yeah, and it looks terrible." I realized I hadn't said those words out loud to anyone, and the realization hit me like that car had.

Teracht tipped his head again, studying me intently with all eight of his eyes, unblinking, which was more than a little disconcerting. "I don't see what's so terrible about it."

I snorted. "Oh, you don't?"

"Caleb, are you angry with me?" The words came out sounding like Teracht might cry.

"No," I said, shoving my hand through my hair in frustration. "I just... you're not like what I thought you'd be."

"What did you think I'd be?" Teracht asked.

I shrugged. "I don't know... More fearsome."

"You wanted to be afraid of me?"

"I-" The words caught in my throat, and I went silent.

Teracht's many eyes narrowed a little, and the effect

was slightly terrifying. "You thought that because I was a monster, I would be evil and might hurt you?"

"I don't know," I said, though I did. I knew exactly what I had thought. I had thought maybe if Teracht had been ugly and cruel and had hurt me, it would make me feel less angry at myself. I could blame him, and every other monster out there, for rejecting me over the thing that made me so upset. That I would realize I was the monster I envisioned every day.

"Well, I'm sorry to disappoint you," Teracht said, his voice surprisingly soft, his eyes a combination of sadness and hurt. "I'm probably one of the few monsters in this world who doesn't have fangs." He curled his lips back so I could see inside his mouth, and I realized he was being literal. He didn't even have teeth at all, it looked like, just a hard protrusion on the top and bottom inside his mouth. "I couldn't bite you even if I wanted to. And anyway, I don't eat humans. None of us do."

I nodded numbly. Of course he didn't. If monsters were killing humans, they wouldn't be signing up for dating apps and living in houses with grocery delivery. The military would be hunting them down and slaughtering them like animals.

"Why do you want to be afraid of me?"

Teracht still sounded hurt, and it burned inside of me like icy fire. "I don't know," I said, hearing the anger in my own voice, but I suddenly felt like I was unable to control it. "I guess I wanted to know what monsters were like. To see if they actually cared about humans." *About me.*

"You can't judge all monsters by one," Teracht said, and I felt guilt tug at my stomach. He was right; it wasn't any different than judging an entire group of people because of one person's skin color or sexual orientation or religion. It wasn't okay. I knew I was being an ass. I didn't want to be. I realized that my first major attempt at socializing since my accident should not have been a date, and especially should not have been a date with a monster when I knew so little about them. I had made a bunch of assumptions, all of which had been wrong.

"Caleb." Teracht's voice was cold, much colder than he had sounded the entire time I had been here. "I wanted to find someone who didn't care that I was a monster. Someone who treated me like... I don't know. But not like this."

Inwardly, I cringed. He was right again. He deserved so much better than me. Someone who was not angry at the world, who had their shit together. "Look, um, I don't think this is going to work," I said, feeling guilt wash over me like a tidal wave. Teracht had been nothing but kind. I knew it was my own hangups that were bothering me. "I'm sorry. I'll just go." I got to my feet, took two steps toward the door, and promptly tripped over absolutely nothing. Both of my arms shot out in front of me on instinct, but I realized too late that I was not going to be able to catch myself with only my one hand. I braced myself to hit the floor face-first.

I had squeezed my eyes shut, but when the impact didn't come, I cautiously peeked them open. The floor was only inches from my nose, but I had not hit it. When I glanced down, I saw several pairs of dark, jointed, spindly legs wrapped around me, from my waist to my knees, and one pair of more human-like arms around my shoulders.

Teracht pulled me upright. "Are you all right?" he asked as I got my feet under me again. I could feel that my face was bright red as he drew back all of his appendages and gazed worriedly at me.

"Um, yeah. Thanks," I said, starting to push my hair out of my face instinctively with my right hand and then quickly switching to my left. "How did you move that fast?"

Teracht smiled sheepishly. "I can move very quickly when I want to. It's how I would catch prey in the other world."

"Oh," I said. That made my skin crawl a little for reasons I didn't want to think about. "You're really strong." I had been falling weight, all 180 pounds of me, and he had caught me like it was nothing, even with those slender legs.

Teracht actually blushed, his cheeks coloring a slightly purple color under his dark skin. "I suppose I am."

"I..." I had to lick my lips that suddenly felt really dry. "How exactly do you catch prey?"

"Well, I don't do it here," Teracht said, sounding a little defensive, and I realized how I must sound.

"No, no!" I shook my head quickly. "Sorry, that came out weird. I was just curious." Teracht hesitated. I could see something in his dark eyes, but I wasn't really sure how to read it. "I'm not going to judge you," I said, hoping that was what was bothering him. "And you don't have to if you don't want to. I was just wondering, is all, since you moved so quick."

Teracht's lips curved into a cautious smile. "Would you like to see?"

"Sure!" The word came out of me before I even thought about it. "That is, if you want to show me."

"Wait here a minute." Teracht turned and scurried away on his eight legs across the hardwood floor. I watched him move in fascination. He was surprisingly fast on his feet, though not as much as I would think to be able to catch me from falling. He moved over to the open concept kitchen, opening the fridge before he returned a moment later, holding a full gallon plastic container of orange juice. At least, I thought that was what it was.

"Hold this," he instructed. I took the container, seeing from the label that I had guessed the contents correctly, which somehow felt reassuring. Teracht suddenly climbed up one of the pieces of webbing anchored to one of the walls, the whole structure vibrating just a little from his weight. He crawled up until he was in the corner of the living room, facing me as he settled into the spot. If we had been in the house of a giant, he would not have looked out of place as a little spider hanging out in the corner of the ceiling. "Toss that at my web."

I glanced down at the container in confusion. "You mean... the whole jug?"

Teracht nodded. "Mm-hmm. Anywhere you like." And then all eight of his dark eyes closed.

I hesitated, feeling extremely weird, but I lifted the jug, glancing around for what seemed to be an area with the least amount of breakable stuff behind it, and underhand tossed the jug into the mess of webbing.

I half expected it to bounce back at me, or even rip through the gossamer strings, but to my surprise, it stuck on the strands that caught it, as easily as if I had tossed it into a net. The next moment, before my eyes could even process what I was seeing, Teracht had shot from the corner, grasping the captured container between his spidery feet, and was winding a silvery-white web around it, turning the container so fast I could barely see it, hearing the juice slosh around inside. Within moments, the entire jug was completely covered in white spider silk, like a cocoon around an orange juice butterfly. Teracht let it go, and it stayed right where he left it, wrapped in the strands, stuck on the webbing that his strange spider legs and body clung to as easily as I stood on the ground. All of this happened in a matter of seconds, and I hadn't even fully realized it was done until Teracht turned to me, a tiny, hopeful smile quirking his lips.

"Wow." I couldn't think of anything else to say for a long moment, just staring at the encapsulated container, imagining if that had been a live creature of some kind. "That was weird. And really cool. And yes, holy damn, you are fucking fast!"

Teracht beamed at that and pointed one spider leg back toward the corner he had started from. "I can cut my web to launch myself at prey. Or, to catch people falling in my doorway," he added, his smile turning a bit more shy. "Not that I've had any need to hunt prey here in your world."

"Yeah, I suppose plastic jugs don't put up much of a fight," I said, and Teracht nodded in amusement. "How big of prey would you catch?"

Teracht blinked, then hummed thoughtfully. "Usually, things smaller than myself, though multiple atauri sometimes work together if it is something larger."

"Are at- uh, those, your species name?" I asked.

"Atauri," Teracht said again. "Yes, that's... well, that's what I'm calling us in your world, since our language doesn't really have the equivalent of human speech."

"What happens after you catch them and wrap them up?" I asked, indicating the small cocoon of orange juice still just hanging out on the webbing.

Teracht's smile faded just a bit. "Well... we can only eat things that are liquid. So we... regurgitate a powerful acid onto the prey to... melt... it?" He sounded uncertain about the exact process, but that was more than enough information for me.

"Got it," I said, sure I was unable to keep my nose from

wrinkling.

Teracht looked like I had kicked him. "Does that bother you, Caleb?"

"What? No," I said quickly. "No, it's just... You do what you gotta do to eat, I suppose."

Teracht nodded. "Yes. But I like your human world. I do not have to hunt for prey. I can have whatever I want delivered."

"Do you regurgitate acid onto your food here?" I asked, not sure if that was a rude question or not.

Teracht actually laughed, the sound surprisingly bright. "No. I only get things that are already liquid. I haven't had to liquefy my own food since arriving here. It has been quite pleasant, actually, and it allows me to conserve energy better."

I couldn't really argue with that. Throwing up stomach acid to dissolve my dinner in order to eat it did not sound pleasant at all. I realized as I stood there that my earlier awkwardness and Teracht's discomfort with me seemed to have faded away, and I didn't feel like fleeing out the door like I had only a few minutes ago. Teracht seemed much more at ease with me, and I with him. I hesitated before glancing over at the couch. "Hey, um, I'm sorry for what I said earlier. It wasn't right, to put you in that position or to assume stuff about you."

Teracht blinked all eight of his eyes together, which for some reason made me smile. "I forgive you," he said slowly.

"We monsters often have assumptions made about us."

"Yeah," I agreed. "I'm starting to know what that feels like."

Teracht cocked his head to the side, which I was noticing he did when he did not understand something. "What do you mean?"

"I..." I swallowed hard, then pointed to the couch. "Can I sit down?"

"Yes, of course," Teracht said with a gracious wave of one of his more human-like hands. I took my spot on the couch again.

"Since the accident, a lot of people make weird assumptions about me too. That I can't hear them or see them when they look at me or whisper about me. Or that because my face is messed up, it means I'm stupid. They talk louder and slower or treat me like a kid." I hadn't yet said these words out loud, but as they came out of my mouth, I felt the weight of them slump my shoulders. "Even the people who know me treat me differently. But I'm still the same person I was before that."

"Are you?" Teracht asked, making his way along one of the lines of webbing to hover next to me like he had earlier.

"Am I what?"

"Are you the same person that you were before you were in your accident?"

I started to say "Yes," but it caught in my throat as I stared into the eight dark eyes holding mine. I swallowed, feeling like a golf ball was suddenly lodged behind my Adams apple. "I... I don't know," I confessed. "I haven't really felt entirely like myself since it happened."

Teracht was silent for a moment before he rested his chin on his folded arms, gazing at me. "I don't know Caleb Webster, either who he was before the accident, or who he is now. Why don't you tell me?"

I blinked in surprise. "Tell you who I am?"

Teracht nodded. "I don't know any differently, so it's not like I will contradict you."

That made a laugh bubble in my chest. "I guess. Um..." I licked my lips slowly, suddenly unsure what I should say. "What do you want to know?"

Teracht thought for a long moment. "What are you most afraid of?"

"Wow, jumping in with both feet here," I couldn't help but mutter, feeling the color flush from my cheeks. Teracht just looked back at me expectantly. I hesitated, fingers tangling into the knees of my pants as I gave some thought to his question. "I know a lot of people are afraid of death. But I don't think I am. At least, I've accepted it's going to happen one day. But I guess..." I looked up into Teracht's eyes, and his expression was kind. "I'm sort of afraid of what's happening to me. That I'm living, but I'm not really living, you know?"

Teracht was silent for a moment, and I wondered if maybe I had confused him, when he spoke up. "You feel trapped.

Like the world is moving without you, and you're missing out on it."

"Yes!" I said, sitting up a little more. "That's it. Ever since the accident, I feel like I'm stuck in one place while everybody else moves on."

Teracht smiled, but it wasn't a happy one. There was something sorrowful in his dark gaze. "There's life to live, but you're afraid to live it, because maybe it's not what you expect?"

Heat flooded my eyes unexpectedly, and I had to take a deep breath to keep the sudden tears from making it past my lashes. "Yeah," I said softly. "Or because *I'm* not what I expect anymore."

Teracht nodded slowly, and he reached out one of his human hands to brush something off of my face with the back of one finger. A tear had broken free and tracked down my cheek. "I know exactly what that feels like," he said. "I came here, to this world, and I've hardly explored any of it. Because what if people are not all right with me? What if I scare people, or do something that makes them think all monsters are bad?"

"I don't think you're scary," I said quietly.

Teracht smiled at that. "I don't want people to be afraid of me. And I don't want to be afraid of people."

"Are you afraid of me?" The words came out before I had even thought about them, and I wished I could drag them back. If Teracht said yes, my worst fear about myself, that I was scary and unlikable, would come true.

Teracht stared at me for a moment before his hand reached out and pressed lightly to my left cheek. "Not at all."

The words broke me in a way I wasn't expecting, and shame flooded me as tears spilled down my cheeks, burning hot on my skin. Teracht frowned and stroked them away with his thumb, being extra gentle as he touched my scarred right cheek. "Why are you crying?" he asked, sounding concerned, as if he had said something to offend me.

I reached up to touch his hand on my cheek. "I don't know."

Teracht stared back at me for a long moment, not moving, before he slid forward, taking both of my cheeks gently in his hands. His one on my scarred right side was feather-light, conscious of not putting pressure on the wounds. "May I kiss you?" he whispered.

"Yes." I didn't move or tear my eyes from him. My heart just picked up a little in my chest, my left hand pressing his hand closer against my cheek.

Teracht leaned in and touched his lips to mine. It was soft and sweet and shy, barely a brush over my mouth, his head angled to press more to the left side than the right. He started to pull back after only a moment, but my hand tightened around his, and he paused. I pressed my own mouth back, keeping it light in return. I hadn't kissed anyone like this since high school, so gentle and innocent, barely a brush between us, our breath mingling on the other's cheek. And it had been so long since I had been touched by another person. I hadn't realized until that moment how much I missed physical contact, and especially more intimate touches than just doctors or physical therapists.

Teracht slowly pulled away, his cheeks a delightful blush, as his hands left my face. "Was that all right?" he asked, ducking his head and biting his lower lip nervously. He had gorgeous lips, I noticed again, now curious if actual spiders had lips too. I was not about to Google that right now though.

I nodded slowly. "Yeah. Thank you."

Chapter 4

Teracht

"MAY I KISS YOU?" I had asked him, even though my instinct was to just lean in and do it. Humans were very concerned with consent, and I did not want to upset Caleb, especially not at this moment. He looked so lost, as if one wrong touch could shatter whatever fragile mask he had built in place since his accident.

He hesitated for a moment before he nodded. "Yes."

My hand on his cheek stayed there as I leaned down and pressed my lips carefully to his. My experience with kissing had been entirely based on what I'd watched on TV, giving my own hand experimental kisses until I figured out the lip position, not completely unlike drinking through a straw, which I often did. So, I was sure it was not an exceptionally good kiss. But Caleb nearly melted into the touch, his left hand sliding up to hold my hand on his face lightly as he kissed me back. This new sensation was strange, sending a soft, pleasant warmth through my body unlike anything I had felt before. Was this why humans liked kissing so much? Did they feel this warm rush throughout their bodies when they touched mouths too?

We held the kiss, which I was pretty sure meant that he liked it. I wasn't sure if it might hurt his injuries, and I certainly did not want to make him feel pain in any way. I shifted a little, trying to put more of the kiss against the left side of his lips.

After a few moments, we did have to pull back to breathe. He moved his hand to brush his fingers over his lips, as if to check if they were still there. I smiled slightly. "Was that all right?"

"Yeah. Thank you," he said. "That was really nice. I... Wow, it's been a while since anyone has touched me like that."

I laughed. "I don't think I have ever touched anyone that way."

"You didn't have a... a girlf... boy... spider-friend in the monster world?" he asked, looking a bit flustered as he tried to figure out how to phrase it.

"No. My kind are not very affectionate," I said. He didn't need to know yet that female spiders often ate their young if they did not flee the nest fast enough when they were born. "And you are the first human I have chosen to spend time with."

He blinked, then gave me a sheepish grin. "And I'm doing such a great job at first impressions."

I shook my head. "It is new for both of us. I have already forgiven you for the things you said when you were angry."

He flushed and looked down. His one hand had curled into the knees of his pants and seemed to be trembling just a bit. "I had no right to be angry at you. I'm sorry again."

"I forgive you again," I said, and he let out a soft snort of laughter, looking up at me. I had not meant it to be funny, but seeing Caleb laugh made me feel good all over. Despite the injuries that he was obviously very self-conscious about, he was still ridiculously handsome, and his smile lit up his whole face.

"You're the first... anything that I've really spent time with since my accident," he admitted. "My mom came to stay when I first got out of the hospital, and a couple friends came over to check on me, but, I don't know, things changed. I think it's like you said, I'm not the same guy I was back in August. Not even just my looks and having to adapt to life with only one hand. My whole life changed. I could have died, but I didn't. And I'm acting like I died anyway."

I hesitated for a moment. "I know that my situation is not the same as yours, but I feel like perhaps I understand, at least a little. I haven't left this house except for a few rare moments. Because..." I took a deep breath and let it out. "Because I am afraid. I am afraid people will judge me, as a monster. They will think I am scary or evil. So, I stay here, because I tell myself it will hurt less to hide alone than to have someone be cruel."

"Fuck." Caleb let out a gasp of air. "Yes, that's what we're both doing. We're hiding from the world because we don't want the world to hurt us."

The fact that humans could be just as cruel to humans who were from there as they could be to monsters who were not made no sense to me. "You think that other humans will judge you for something that you can't control?" I asked.

"Yeah," he said with a bit of scoff, though I knew he wasn't trying to be mean. "Unfortunately, a lot of humans suck. They don't like people who are different. Who are ugly or damaged."

"I don't think you are either of those things," I said and meant every word of it. My hand reached out to cover his left that was still clutching his pants leg. "I think you are hurting and angry, which is understandable."

He looked up in surprise at my touch, but his hand shifted to curl into mine. After a moment, he lifted the stump of his right forearm and laid it on the top of my hand holding his, his ocean blue eyes watching me. I wondered if it was a test of some kind, to see how I would react to his injury touching me. It hurt me to think that his touch might have repulsed someone else, that they might have pulled away from someone who was obviously in pain and in desperate want of connection. I reached up my other hand to rub lightly at the scarred stump, careful not to catch his skin with my pointed fingertips. "I am not afraid of you."

Caleb swallowed hard. "You're not?"

"Why would I be? You were in an accident. What happened was awful, and I can't imagine how much pain it has caused you. But I do not want to be a source of pain for you, or you for me."

Caleb turned his eyes up to mine, and I could see what looked like tears forming in them again. "Teracht..."

"Please don't cry," I said quickly, afraid I had messed up and said something I shouldn't have. "I don't want you to be sad."

"Sorry," he said, pulling his right arm away to swipe at his eyes. "It's not you. God, it's not you." He took a deep breath, his fingers on his left hand curling around mine. "It's just been so long since I've felt anything except angry and bitter. I don't want to feel that way. And you're making me feel things."

"I'm sorry," I said, starting to draw my hand away, albeit reluctantly, but he held tight to it.

"No, not... I don't want you to stop. I... I like you touching me. It's been so long since anyone touched me."

I smiled softly, brushing my hand very lightly up his right forearm toward his shoulder. "I would like to touch you and see all of you."

"I haven't let anyone see my body except for doctors and my mom since the accident," Caleb said.

I hesitated. An idea had been forming in my mind that I hadn't given much thought to, figuring it would be too much of an ask for a new relationship. But Caleb had been more receptive to some things than I had expected. It might be worth asking, and I certainly would not be upset if he said no. "I have a thought, if you're interested."

"Shoot," he said.

I blinked all eight of my eyes. "Does that mean tell you?"

"Sorry. Yes," he replied with a small chuckle. "Tell me."

I licked my lips with the tip of my tongue, and it did not escape my notice that he watched the movement. "I am not overly familiar with human bodies. And I'm sure you are curious about mine as well."

He nodded slowly, waiting for me to continue.

"Could we... perhaps-" My words were getting stuck now as I realized how strange my request was going to sound, maybe even creepy. "Never mind."

"Oh, come on," Caleb prompted. "Just say what you're thinking."

I let out a quick breath. "What if we just took time to look at each other and touch each other?" I said in a bit of a rush.

Caleb stared, and I felt my face heat, ducking my head.

"Like, you touch me, and I touch you?" he asked.

"Something like that," I said softly.

Caleb was quiet for a moment, and I waited for him to get upset or tell me how inappropriate that suggestion was. From what I understood, humans did not just go around touching people they barely knew. So, it surprised me when he said, "Okay, yeah."

I knew all eight of my eyes were wide. "Really?"

He nodded. "Yeah. I mean, I'm curious how all this," he gestured to me with his hand, "works. So, I guess it would only be fair to let you, you know, look at me." His voice dropped a little. "If it really doesn't bother you."

"It doesn't," I tried to reassure him. I was pretty sure he was much more concerned about how he looked than I was, but even after only a few hours of conversation, I had a much better understanding of how important Caleb's appearance was to him, and what it had meant to him.

Caleb nodded slowly. "Okay. But let's save that for the next date? I probably should get home before it gets too dark."

I felt a flutter in my chest. We were going on a second date! Despite our rocky start, things seemed to be going well, and he was the one suggesting getting together again. "Very well," I said congenially, bobbing my head. "When should we get together?"

"How about I'll text you," Caleb suggested, and I nodded.

"All right. Shall I get your jacket?"

"Please." Caleb rose to his feet, stretching a little. I moved past him to the closet to retrieve his coat. I held it open for him. He blinked in surprise, then smiled. "Thanks."

"Of course." I held the jacket until he had slid both of his arms inside of it, then draped his scarf around his neck. He zipped up the front before taking the scarf and wrapping it around his face so it was hidden, as he had been on my doorstep only a few hours ago. "It was very nice to meet you, Caleb."

"It was nice to meet you too, Teracht," he said, and I could hear the smile in his voice even if I couldn't see it through the scarf.

I opened the door, a chilly blast of late winter air greeting us. The sun was already starting to sink in the sky, and everything looked a little gray. "Please text me when you get home so I know you are safe?"

"I will, thanks. I'll talk to you again soon." Then he stepped into the dying sunlight, down the path, through the gate to the sidewalk. I watched him go until he turned the corner and was lost from view. Only then did I close and lock the door.

Chapter 5

Caleb

I texted Teracht when I walked in my apartment door after a quick bus ride home, letting him know I had made it and thanking him for a nice first date. He responded almost immediately, saying he was glad I was safe and that he enjoyed our date as well.

I didn't text him for a few days after that. There was a strange itch in the back of my mind that wanted to know how he was doing, if he was thinking about me. Our first meeting had been odd, but Teracht was nicer than I had imagined he would be, especially considering how much of an ass I had been to him at first and how rude he could have been to me in return. But it also felt a little overwhelming. Meeting a monster, who shared some of my same feelings and fears, who barely ever left the house because of how people might perceive him, was a whole lot of new to deal with, on top of going on a date or really even socializing with another person since my accident. I wasn't sure how to process all of this, so I avoided talking to Teracht for several days. I wondered if he might text me instead, but he did not, and I wondered if he was trying to respect my privacy until I was ready to talk.

It was Wednesday morning before I finally texted him.

CALEB: Hey. Sorry I haven't messaged you. I had a lot to think about but I'm doing better now.

I wasn't sure how quickly he would text me back. I kept checking my phone, but I did not get a reply. I took a shower and ate some lunch, but I still did not hear from him for several more hours. It was late in the afternoon, and I had checked my phone probably a hundred times by then, before I got a text back. My heart did an excited little hop in my chest when I heard the buzz.

TERACHT: I'm glad you are doing all right. Did you still want to get together again?

I debated playing it cool and waiting a bit before I texted him back, but I decided I was not going to play those kinds of games with Teracht. He had been so hopeful in finding someone to talk to, I couldn't continue to leave him hanging.

CALEB: Yeah I'd like that. U free on Sat?
TERACHT: Yes all day.
CALEB: Did you still want to do that touching thing?
TERACHT: Yes. If you are still all right with it.
CALEB: Yeah. Should I come over for lunch?

There was a pause before Teracht responded, and I wondered if he was trying to interpret that beyond the basic message. But then he replied.

TERACHT: Is it all right that I only consume liquids?
CALEB: I can bring my own food if thats cool with u.
TERACHT: If it would not be too much trouble.
CALEB: No trouble. Should I bring something for you too?
TERACHT: No thank you.
CALEB: OK. 11?
TERACHT: See you then!

Saturday morning, I packed my lunch bag, which I had not used in almost a year, with an ice pack to keep everything chilled, and slid in a simple sandwich, chips, and some fruit. No reason to get fancy with my meal when we were going to be at his house. I also wasn't sure if I would feel like eating much as I prepared myself for what was ahead. Teracht wanted to see me. All of me. Naked and under his touch. I wondered what those spider-like legs would feel like on my skin, since I hadn't touched them skin to skin yet. He and I had not touched that much, but every press of his hands against my cheek or my arm had been like coming into a warm room from a blizzard. And I wanted more of that feeling.

I gave in and propped up one of my mirrors in the bathroom. I took extra care with grooming that morning, shaving all of the stubble on my face off (only on the left, I was pretty sure my scarred right half would never grow hair again,) plucking a few stray eyebrow hairs, and giving my junk a careful once-over to trim the hair down. I was not feeling confident about giving myself a full-on shave with only one hand yet, and I really did not want to end up in the emergency room explaining I had taken a testicle off in preparation to get naked for my monster date. I had started up a skincare routine again when I had joined the Monster Match app. I had to be gentle on my scars and use a few alternate products so my wounds did not sting or pull.

I smoothed a soothing gel over the scar on my cheek, studying it in the mirror as I did. I still hated it. I hated everything about how my face looked now. Even my unblemished left half made me angry because it reminded me of what I no longer had. I would give anything to go back to that day in August, to leave the house a minute earlier or later, to be going just a little faster or slower through that intersection. But what was done was done. I finished putting some product in my hair, the first time I had done so since before my accident. And then I wiped the rest of the sticky mess over my reflection in the mirror.

Once I was on the bus, I texted him that I was on my way and received a smiley face emoji in return. My scarf was still wrapped securely around my face, shoulders hunched against the cold. I turned the corner onto his block and approached the house with less caution than I had last time. I rang the bell, and the door opened almost immediately, no lock clicking beforehand. Teracht smiled at me as he held the door open. "Hello, Caleb."

"Hi," I said, stepping inside, glad to leave the chill behind.

"My delivery got here just before you," Teracht said, gesturing me inside and holding out his hands for my coat. "I was putting it away."

"Oh. Do you need any help?" I offered.

"No, thank you," he said. I set down my lunch bag before undoing my jacket and scarf, handing them to him. He put them in the closet as I pulled off my slide-on boots.

Teracht glanced down at my lunch bag. "Shall I take that for you?"

"Sure." I picked it up and handed it to him, and he moved toward the kitchen. "Please, sit. I'll be right back."

I moved to the sofa, which looked like it had not been used at all since my last visit. I sat down, gazing around the room at the tangle of webs that stretched high into the vaulted ceiling above me. There probably was some sort of order or design to it, but I couldn't see what it was. I glanced over, not able to see into Teracht's fridge too easily with him standing in front of it, but I heard things being shifted around, and a muttered hissing sound that I thought might be a curse in Teracht's monster language. "You sure you don't need help?"

"I got it," Teracht replied, and a few moments later, the fridge door closed, and he was making his way back over to me. He glanced at the other side of the couch before gingerly shifting to settle on it with his large hind end draping over the arm, his spidery legs tucked underneath him like a giant cat. I wasn't sure if he was comfortable or not like that. "How have you been?"

"All right," I said. "You?"

"All right," he echoed.

"I'm sorry I didn't text you earlier in the week," I said. "I just... I had a lot to think about, and it was a little overwhelming."

Teracht nodded solemnly. "I understand. You gave me a lot to think about too."

"Did I?" I asked curiously.

"Yes." Teracht blinked his humanoid set of eyes as he gazed at me. "But you are not overwhelmed now?"

"Not as much," I said. "Though I'm a little nervous about today."

"Why?" Teracht asked, tipping his head slightly. I was still fascinated by how his hair stayed straight up.

"I dunno. I guess if we're going to do the touching each other thing."

"Yes," Teracht said. "If you still want to."

"Yeah, I do. I'm just... It's been a really long time since anyone has seen me without clothes, and not since– not while my body has looked like this."

Teracht nodded again. "I do not wish for you to be uncomfortable, Caleb. If you don't want to, we do not have to."

"I want to," I said quickly. "I do. It will just be a little adjustment for me."

"Would you like to touch me first?"

"Would that be all right?"

"Of course. Now?"

"I guess now is as good a time as any," I chuckled nervously. Teracht got off the couch with the grace of someone who did not know how to get off of a couch, moving to stand in the middle of the open floor.

"Tell me what you'd like me to do, but go ahead and touch me if you'd like," he said.

I hesitated. This suddenly felt super weird, but it wasn't exactly like I learned atauri anatomy in high school. "Can I touch your legs?"

"Of course!" Teracht held out one of his front appendages to me. I opened my palm, and he carefully placed it in my hand, like a dog learning to shake. My fingers closed around it and stroked lightly. It was softer than I expected, with a very fine layer of some sort of hair over it, like an antler. But it also was not heavy. I had been expecting something similar to solid steel, but it felt surprisingly delicate under my touch, more like a dowel.

"Wow, that's not what I was expecting," I said. "They're really light."

He nodded. "They are. But they are actually quite strong."

"Yeah, I suppose they have to be. Why are all your legs on your middle and not on your back end?"

Teracht glanced behind him, gazing at his round hindquarters with no legs. "Flexibility, perhaps. I never really thought about it before," he said, bending slightly where the segments came together, as if experimenting with his own movement. "It looks heavy, but it really is not."

"I can't break them or anything?" I asked as I held his slender spider leg, wondering if I could hurt him if I squeezed too hard.

Teracht smiled a bit. "Not easily. I believe they are similar to the bones in your arms and legs. They could be broken, but it would take the right angle and a lot of force."

"Is your whole body like that?" I asked, reaching out my hand to place it lightly on his chest. He froze, and I yanked my hand back as if I had burned him. "Sorry! I shouldn't touch without asking!"

"No, I... Do it again," Teracht said, his voice oddly soft. I reached out my hand and pressed it to his chest. If I hadn't been able to see it, I would guess that I was touching the outside of a suit of armor, though one that was warmer than metal.

Teracht was quiet, but I could see his tension visibly fade away throughout his body at my touch. I wondered if anyone had actually ever touched him like this before. "Is this all right?"

Teracht nodded, and I let my hand slide over the plane of his chest, down toward where the round middle piece started to swell. If he had been human, I would have figured my hand was resting just below his navel, though he didn't have one of those. And below that was just a flat transition into his middle abdomen. I felt my face heat as I cautiously ventured, "So, um... Do you have a dick?"

I swear Teracht's entire human form turned pink. "Yes, I do," he said, his voice low. "But it's not there. And it's not meant to... for..."

Teracht blushing was ridiculously cute. "What? Come on, we're both guys here, and this is for educational purposes anyway."

"I do not believe it's designed to fit with human anatomy," Teracht said quickly. "Even in the monster world, we don't really use them the way that humans do."

"How do you use it then?" I asked, oddly curious now.

His blush got deeper. "Our penises do not have much sensation in them. We stick it inside of the female, and it breaks off with the sperm still inside of it."

"Ouch." I couldn't stop a flinch. Spider sex did not sound very romantic. Really, talk of breaking things during sex didn't sound fun in any way. "Uh, you said it's not there." I waved my hand in the general vicinity of where his groin would be, trying to move on from the very uncomfortable feeling between my legs. "Where is it?"

"Um..." I swear that none of his eight eyes were looking at me.

"Fuck, I'm sorry," I said, rubbing at my face with my hand. How fucking rude could I be, demanding he whip out his monster dick? "You don't have to show me anything, I was just curious."

Teracht let out a soft sound that might have been a laugh in his throat. "It pleases me that you are so curious," he said. "I will show it to you, but maybe later? If that's all right?"

"Yeah, of course, no problem," I said, letting my eyes roam over his segmented body again. Moving along when both of us were obviously uncomfortable felt like the best option. "Can I keep touching you? I'm curious what your... fur? feels like."

Teracht hummed softly in amusement. "I believe it is more like hair than fur. But you can keep touching, and perhaps you can tell me."

"Okay," I said, glancing down at the bulbous parts. "Let me know if I'm about to touch anything I shouldn't."

Teracht made another sound. I couldn't figure out if it was laughter or something else, but he held still for my hand to travel down his stomach, over the ridges there, and then brush the swollen middle part of him where his legs all connected. He inhaled but did not move. It was firm like muscle beneath my touch, and he was right in that what looked like fur was almost more like hair. It was sleek and fairly soft, though very tough. My hand traced over it, then to a spot where one of his legs attached to his middle. He gave a little squirm, and I realized in delight that he was ticklish there. I filed that away for later, not wanting to take advantage of his trust with this first exploration.

I took a few steps to the side, watching Teracht for any sign of discomfort, but he held still except for turning his head slightly to watch me as I moved around him, letting my hand brush over the larger back segment of his body that had no legs to support it. This too felt very strong, though a little hollower and much lighter than I had expected, almost like a water balloon. I wasn't sure he would appreciate the comparison though, so I kept that to myself, tracing my fingers over the fine patterns of the hair there, which I figured must be to camouflage him in dim light. "These are kind of neat. Do all atauri have these markings?"

Teracht nodded. "Yes. Each one is different, and some are more subtle than others. I am not as flashy as some others of my kind."

I wondered how many other kinds of spider creatures there were. I knew there were a ton of different spider species on Earth, though some of them were exclusive to specific places. I trailed my fingers over the marks, towards the tapered end of his... hindquarters? I wasn't sure what to call it as I took another step to see him better from the back. At the end of that bulbous part was a strange sort of mound with six little raised areas on them. I reached out my hand to touch them, and Teracht jumped. "Sorry," I said quickly. "Did I hurt you?"

He shook his head. "It is all right. Those are my spinnerets. Maybe don't touch those, there are a lot of intricacies there, and they are a little sensitive."

"Yeah, no problem," I said. "I'd love to see how they work sometime though."

Teracht nodded. "I will spin for you later if you'd like," he offered.

"Great!" I said, examining the spot with just my eyes instead. Each of the six areas looked like they were covered with some sort of little hairs or barbs. I had never had a reason to look closely at the back end of a spider before. "How many kinds of webbing can you create?"

Teracht looked thoughtful. "I don't really know," he said. "I have quite a few different types, and many of them can be combined together as well."

"How does your body know which one to do?" I asked.

"I push an internal button," Teracht said. I blinked and turned to look at him. His face was deadly serious before he broke into a fit of giggles. "I'm sorry, bad joke."

I snickered too, picturing tiny little spiders inside of him hitting a button in a factory to change the type of webbing.

"I couldn't tell you exactly how I do it," Teracht said. "It's instinctual. But I'm sure it has to do with proteins and other things mixing a certain way for each one."

I was even more curious about his webbing now, but I supposed it might be rude to keep lingering on it when he had promised to show me later, so I just went back to my exploration. The pattern on his hind end was very interesting, and it felt strange but rather nice to trace my fingers over it. I crossed back around to the front of him, and he gazed at me with his unblinking eyes. "Can I touch your ears and hair?" I asked curiously.

"Yes." Teracht lowered himself to the floor to rest on his haunches like a cat doing loaf, inclining his head toward me. His ears were smaller than mine and did not have the cartilage shaping them that mine did, but they were surprisingly cute, and I ran my fingers over the lobe of one. Teracht made a soft noise almost like a purr.

"Your ears are small compared to human ones," I said, stroking it again.

"Yes. My hearing is similar to that of humans, I would think," he said. "I do not rely on it as my main sense for hunting."

I nodded, then slid my hand up to brush lightly through his hair. It felt similar to the hair on his spider body. "Does your hair stay up naturally like this?" I asked, finding I could move it around a little bit, but it still stayed sticking straight up.

"Yes," Teracht said. "My hair is made from a similar protein as my webbing."

"I like this look," I said, running my fingers through it. "I wish I could get my hair to do that naturally. I would make millions."

"Oh?" Teracht asked, tipping his head.

"Back when I was modeling. Getting hair to do cool stuff wasn't the easiest and would require a lot of shots and time to get it looking right. I know a couple art directors who would kill to have my hair stand up naturally like this."

Teracht smiled, reaching up his segmented fingers to run them through my blond almost-shoulder-length hair. "I like your hair," he said, tangling a bit of it around his finger. "It's beautiful."

I blushed but held still for him to touch it. I was used to people touching my hair anyway, and this felt like a pretty natural transition into him exploring me. His humanoid fingers ran through my hair, grazing my scalp lightly, then moved from my hairline to my face. He examined my ears closely and peered curiously into my eyes, his own dark ones unnervingly close to me as he did. I realized as I stared back into my own reflection in them that each of his eyes had a small eyelid that allowed it to blink, though they very rarely did, and they did not all necessarily blink at the same time. "Is your vision really good with so many eyes?" I asked curiously.

"Hmm? Not as much as you would think," Teracht said, pulling back just a bit and waving his hand in the air around him. "It's better than a human's, with more lateral and vertical range. I can see almost all the way behind me without turning my head. But I am also more sensitive to light than a human would be."

"Oh, do you not normally keep the lights on in here?" I asked.

"Not often, though I had dimmers installed so I can control them to a comfortable level."

"Is this bothering you?" I asked, inclining my head at the airy, light-filled room.

"No, I'm fine," Teracht reassured me, drawing my attention back to his lips. God, his lips were gorgeous.

"Can I see your... teeth?"

In response, Teracht curled back his lips and opened his mouth for me to peer inside. He had a tongue similar to a human one, though a little more slender and curled upward at the edges, like his own natural straw. I tried not to think too much about that, in either a good way or a prey way. His mouth was shaped similar inside to a human one as well. As he had shown me on our first date, his 'teeth' were a hard, flat shell on the top and bottom of his mouth in a similar shape to teeth and seemed to be made of the same material as his legs. "So, can you chew things?" I asked as I peered at them.

"No," Teracht said, and he actually sounded a little disappointed. "My jaws are actually weaker than yours. I could crush small things like soft fruit, but my diet is better served as liquid.”

“What kind of liquid?” I asked curiously. “Do you like, drink blood?”

“I could, but in this world, I don’t. I drink many liquids, but mostly sports drinks and fruit juices. I mix protein powders into most everything too.”

“What about coffee and soda?” I asked.

Teracht made a face. “The bubbles of soda are strange. Coffee is bitter, and I like sweet things.”

I tried to imagine what surviving on an all-liquid diet would be like. I knew some people did it, and it was unfortunately not uncommon amongst models trying to lose weight and maintain their figure. “Do you have to pee a lot with all that liquid?”

That made Teracht laugh. “No. Most of it is converted into the various elements I use for spinning. I do expel waste for things that do not get processed though.”

Okay, so spider creatures did poop. I was curious, but that felt like a little too intimate to ask about. So, I just nodded. “You are really cool.”

Teracht blinked his human set of eyes. “I am?”

“Yeah. I mean, you’re a giant spider. You spin webs and can climb on the walls and have really awesome skin. That’s all pretty cool.”

He smiled shyly. “Thank you, Caleb.”

I nodded, then jumped a little as his hands caught my face

and pressed a soft kiss to my lips. It only lasted a moment before he pulled back again. "May I look at you now?"

"Yeah," I said. "Um, should I get naked?"

"Do you want to be naked?" Teracht asked.

I hesitated. My lower half was mostly undamaged from the accident, save for a few small scars on my right hip and thigh; the brunt of the glass, metal, and heat had caught my ribs, arm, neck, and face. Other than in surgery or in the shower, I was never naked anymore, and especially not in front of someone else.

Teracht seemed to sense my uneasiness. "It is all right if you do not want to."

"I just... it's not pretty," I said, gesturing to my right side. That was probably obvious to him from my face and the part of my neck that he could see.

"But it is you," Teracht said.

How did he keep saying things that were so sweet? "You won't be grossed out?"

"Caleb, I came from the monster world where I captured live prey and dissolved them with stomach acid." He somehow said that with a completely straight face.

"Well, when you put it like that," I said, giving him a small smile. I sat down on the couch to slide off my socks, then work my shirt over my head. It took me a little while with only my one hand, but I had started to wear baggy clothes to keep the fabric from rubbing right on my scarring, so it was loose and easy to pull off. I slid off the sweatpants I had been wearing, taking my boxer briefs with it. I set all my clothes into a pile on the other side of the couch before I rose to my feet to stand in front of Teracht without a stitch of clothing on, relying on my old modeling skills to hold still and not fidget.

Teracht watched me, his face betraying nothing about how he felt. Thankfully, it was warm in here, so I wasn't uncomfortable temperature-wise. "May I touch you?" Teracht asked, drawing closer, so close that I could feel the warmth coming off of him.

"Yes," I said. He leaned in close and inhaled. I was suddenly very glad I had taken a long shower this morning. "Is your sense of smell pretty good?"

"Mm, probably better than yours," Teracht said, trailing his hands down my left arm before lifting it to examine my armpit curiously. "But it's not all connected through my nose. I can also smell with my tongue and my legs."

"Weird," I commented, and he laughed. One of his front legs suddenly reached up and traced my armpit and down my ribs to my hip. I had not been expecting it, and it tickled, making me laugh and twist a little. "Hey."

Teracht instantly let go and drew back, and I sobered. "No, sorry, it's fine. I'm just a little ticklish, I guess. Your spider feet feel weird."

"Do they bother you?" Teracht asked.

"No," I said quickly. "You're good. I just wasn't ready for that. But it's fine now."

Teracht looked uncertain. I sighed. "I'm sorry, it's really all right, I promise." I raised my left arm again to bare the skin he had touched earlier.

Teracht hesitated, then slowly moved in and gently ran his spider leg over the spot, making me twitch a little from the sensation but not pull away. It wasn't unpleasant, though I couldn't say it was the best thing I had ever felt either. Teracht examined every inch of the skin of my ribs and hip on my left side, moving down to the side of my thigh, my knee, then had me lift my foot to examine each of my toes individually while I leaned lightly on his shoulder for balance. His spider legs occasionally followed the trail of his human fingers, and I wondered what sort of scents and signals he was getting from me.

After my foot had been thoroughly examined, Teracht moved around behind me. That made the hair on the back of my neck prickle and my skin break out in goosebumps. My body knew there was something predatory behind me that I couldn't see. But he just continued the exploration of my body with his fingers and legs, tracing from the back of my neck, down my spine, feeling my ribs from behind. And then his hands slid down to trace over the globe of my left ass cheek. I jumped. I had been expecting it, but still, suddenly having someone touch me there after so long was weird.

"Did I hurt you?" Teracht asked worriedly.

"No," I said, letting out a breath. "No, you're good. I just... It's been a while since anyone has touched my ass."

"Should I not touch it?" he asked.

"No," I said quickly again. "It's fine."

"Your ass is more intimate than your other body parts, yes?" Teracht asked.

"Yes," I said, realizing that other than his spinnerets, Teracht hadn't seemed all that concerned about where my hands had traveled on him. Maybe spider creatures weren't as sexually driven as humans? I realized now too that he had not shown me his spider dick, but I wasn't about to interrupt his exploration.

Teracht's touch on me continued, but it was softer now as he kneaded his fingers into the glute muscles of my left cheek, then the right. His finger slid down the crease between them, making me shiver. Then his thumbs slid into the crack and pulled my ass cheeks apart surprisingly gently. Though I yelped and nearly shot two stories above my head to the ceiling like a cartoon cat when one of his spider feet brushed over my hole.

Teracht pulled back from me in surprise at the noise and movement. "Are you all right?"

"Yeah," I said, turning to him, my cheeks flushed with embarrassment, realizing that somewhere along the lines of him massaging my butt cheeks, my dick had decided someone wanted to play and was already half-hard. "That's just very intimate and sensitive, probably like your spinner things."

"I'm sorry," he said, looking guilty, and I shook my head

quickly, not liking that look on him.

"No, it's fine! I just... uh... Can we come back to that?"

"Yes, of course," Teracht said, concern still written all over his face. "Do you want to stop?"

"No," I said quickly. "No, it's fine. It's just been a while since I've– since anyone's been down there, and it's just kind of awkward."

He didn't look entirely clear on the situation, but he nodded, glancing over my form. "May I touch your wounds?" he asked, gesturing to my puckered and discolored skin on my right side.

I nodded slowly, taking a deep breath. I hadn't allowed anyone who wasn't my mom or one of my doctors to touch that skin before. "Yeah."

"I will stop if you want me to," Teracht said, his voice gentle. His fingers slid to trace over the large, burned patch on my shoulder. "Does it hurt?"

"A little," I said. "It's sensitive sometimes, but not always, and sometimes it hurts for no reason. But you're not hurting me," I added when he seemed like he might pull away. Teracht's fingers on my damaged skin suddenly felt more intimate than his touches on my ass. He touched my skin almost reverently, fingers caressing, pressing just a bit firmer in a few places but not enough to hurt me, as if checking to see where the sensation started or ended. He lifted the end of my right arm with its scarred stump, his fingers moving over it as he caressed it, then lifted my left hand up to compare it to my right.

"Has it been hard?" he asked, running his fingers over the end again. "Adapting without your hand?"

I nodded slowly. "Yeah, it has. I was right-handed too. The doctors said that I'm a good candidate for a prosthetic, but they don't want to do anything yet because my burns are still healing."

"What is a pro... proshtic?" Teracht asked.

"A prosthetic," I said, and he echoed the word back to me with a grateful nod. "It's a fake hand. I know the technology has come a long way. It used to be that you'd just have a hand, or like a hook or something."

"Like Captain Hook in Peter Pan?" Teracht asked curiously, and I nodded.

"Yeah, something like that."

Teracht beamed. "I think you would look nice as a pirate."

I laughed. "Well, thanks. I'd probably end up taking out my own eye if I actually had a hook for a hand though."

"Will you eventually get a pros... prosthetic?" Teracht asked, pronouncing the word carefully and hitting the consonants in his slightly sharp way.

"I don't know," I said, glancing down at where my forearm ended. "It would probably make some things easier." I caught my lower lip with my teeth. A prosthetic hand was something that I could potentially hide or even use in modeling. Some of those diversity casting directors would shit themselves to get a former model with a robotic arm. But not with the burns on my face and neck. Disability had to be inspirational, overcoming hardship to become "normal" again. I wasn't going to be "normal." My face was always going to be scarred. Maybe it would fade a little over time, but it was deep, and I suspected my mouth and eye would start to droop badly as I got older and lost elasticity in even my healthy skin. That was not inspirational. It was not something people wanted to look at. If I was being honest, it was ugly. And people didn't like ugly. It made them uncomfortable. It made *me* uncomfortable.

"Caleb." Teracht said my name in a way that pulled me from the spiral my mind had started to slide down.

"Yeah, sorry. Thinking too much."

"Do you want to stop?"

"No, no," I said, shaking my head. "I'm fine."

Teracht gestured to the sofa. "Why don't you lay down? I can look at your front that way."

I nodded and moved to stretch out on the couch, tucking one of the decorative pillows under my head. Teracht hovered next to me, and I felt like Sleeping Beauty for a minute, with him gazing down like he wanted to kiss me to wake me up. But then his fingers traced down my puckered neck, brushing my chin, my Adams apple, the hollow at the base of my throat, then down between my pecs.

His fingers traced over my chest, stopping at my right nipple before brushing his fingers over it curiously. I inhaled softly, and he closed his thumb and forefinger around it, giving it a light pinch. I couldn't stop a moan, quickly pressing my hand to my mouth to muffle it. He looked up at me. "Does that feel good?"

"Yeah," I said, trying to send a message to my dick that now was not the time to join the party.

"Female humans have nipples to nurse their young," Teracht said thoughtfully. "But you are not female and would not produce milk. So why do you have them?"

"I don't really know," I said. "I think it's some sort of biological holdover from conception or something. Do female atauri nurse their young?"

"Oh no," Teracht said with a dark chuckle. "We are born with the ability to dissolve and consume the same food as adults."

"Do you have siblings?" I asked curiously as Teracht gave my nipple an experimental tug, moving it back and forth carefully. I was losing the war with my dick and was fighting the urge now to cover it with my hand, not sure if drawing attention to it made it better or worse.

"Many," he said. "But we are not a family unit the way you would think of a family. There is no bonding between parent and child, or between siblings."

Teracht's fingers moved to my other nipple, giving it a harder pinch, and I winced. "Ow."

"Sorry," he said, pulling back with a blush.

"It's fine," I said, smiling reassuringly. "Maybe just treat them like you would your spinners."

He nodded. "I can do that." And then his fingers were tracing down my chest and over my abs. Seven months of surgeries, hospital stays, and physical therapy had not given me much opportunity to exercise or eat really healthy the way I used to to maintain my body. I used to go to the gym frequently, and that had completely stopped. But I was determined I was not going to lose the definition of my abs that I had strived so hard to achieve in my teenage years and maintained through my twenties. I at least worked out at home, and it seemed to be paying off. Teracht's fingers dipped into my belly button curiously. "What exactly does this do?"

"Nothing, really," I said as his finger poked at it, though not pressing too hard. "When babies are in the womb, it's how we're connected to our mothers to get oxygen and food and stuff. When we're born, the cord falls off."

"Fascinating. I shall have to find a documentary about human fetal development," Teracht said, circling my belly button once more with his finger before sliding it out and lower, toward the manicured patch of blond hair at the base of my dick. Despite pleading with myself to behave, it was half-hard again from Teracht playing with my nipples.

"This is sensitive as well?" Teracht asked, nodding at my cock.

"Yeah. Be really gentle with that," I said, suddenly imagining getting my dick ripped off by super spider strength. Not a sexy thought.

"But I can touch it?" he asked, glancing over at me.

I nodded. "Yeah, go ahead."

He turned back to it and brushed his fingers carefully over the tip. My cock gave a twitch. He seemed intrigued, touching it again before wrapping his hand around it and moving it carefully up and down and then side to side like a joystick, each movement cautious and small. His fingers slid down to my balls, brushing over them, and I exhaled softly, squirming a bit. It had been way too long since anyone had touched my balls, and he cupped them curiously with his palm. My legs instinctively spread a bit, and he lifted my sac to peer curiously at the spot underneath it. Despite the clinical approach of it, it had been almost nine months since I'd had sex, and, since my accident, I'd masturbated maybe three times at most. Having hands on my junk felt good, even if the touches were light and uncertain.

One of his spider legs came up to brush over my dick, which sent a weird sort of primal fear through me, but I relaxed after a second, letting him explore. He slid his finger between my ass cheeks and pressed very lightly at my hole again. I groaned, my eyes closing for a moment. He glanced up at me. "Am I hurting you?" he asked.

"No," I said, opening my eyes quickly. "Feels good."

He nodded, and then he suddenly pulled back, all touch gone from my body. I bit my lip as I kept back a sound of disappointment. I guessed the exploration was over.

"Thank you," Teracht said as I sat up. "Your body is

fascinating."

"Yours is too," I said. My dick was fully hard between my legs now, and I wanted to stroke it, but that was not what we were doing right now. He didn't seem to think anything strange of it as he drew back.

"Are you hungry? Should we eat?"

I laughed weakly, trying to distract myself. "Um, yeah, sure."

"I'll grab our food while you get dressed."

"Sounds good," I said, and Teracht headed for the kitchen area. I stared down at my dick, willing it to stop having a mind of its own right now as I pulled on my shirt and boxer briefs and then my sweatpants, not worrying about my socks. Teracht's hardwood floors seemed very clean. He said he didn't spend a lot of time on the ground, but I supposed when he did, he'd want to be able to move easily. And, aside from the webs covering nearly every surface, everything seemed very clean.

Teracht returned to me with my lunch bag in one hand and an open jug of raspberry lemonade in the other; I could see some bits of powder swirling in it still, like he had just mixed protein powder in. I wondered if we used the same stuff. "Would you like to watch something?" he asked, gesturing to the large TV mounted on the wall nearby, the only part of that wall that was not covered in webbing.

"Sure," I said with a grin. "What's your favorite movie?"

He flushed a little. "The first movie I saw when I came to

your world was The Avengers."

"It's a good movie. Let's watch it," I said, and he happily turned on the large screen and settled slightly above me on his web with his lunch as I made myself comfortable on the couch with mine.

Chapter 6

Teracht

We finished lunch and the movie in contented silence. I watched Caleb the whole time with one of my eyes. He seemed focused on the television, but the relaxed slant of his shoulders was great to see. It had been extremely nice of him to let me explore his body, especially with no clothes on, after only knowing each other for a short time and with how much I knew his injuries bothered him. I had found a bunch of pictures of him online, everything from stock photos to clothing modeling and billboards. He had been stunning. He was still stunning, as far as I was concerned. But humans were strangely obsessed with their outer appearance. Even I realized that people on television and in movies were more attractive than the average person walking down the street. And his body had been how he made his living. In a strange way, I was doing that too. If my ability to create my webbing was suddenly taken away, I knew I would lose a large part of my identity and be at a loss of what to do next.

Caleb moved to the kitchen to throw away his trash, and I could see him eyeing my excessively large recycling container with all of my empty bottles in it. "Can I use your bathroom?"

I nodded and pointed down the hall. He headed into it, closing the door. I hoped he wasn't about to leave. Just having him here, even if we were quietly watching a movie, was nice. I was so often alone. But I also couldn't assume that he wanted to continue to see me either. After a minute, Caleb came back and sat down on the couch, raising a brow at me. "Well, now what?"

"I don't know," I admitted. "We had lunch and a movie."

"Yeah. Are you going to try to get into my pants now?"

I am certain my entire body turned bright red. Caleb laughed. "Calm down, Teracht, I'm just joking," he said. "Although, you have seen me naked already."

I ducked my head slightly. "Was that inappropriate of me for only a second date?"

"No," Caleb said, shrugging. "I would have said something if I was concerned about it."

I nodded, my face still burning. "Well, um... Do you have to leave soon?"

Caleb shook his head. "No. But I don't want to overstay my welcome either, so if it's time for me to go, you can tell me."

"No. I like having you here," I said, giving him a small smile, hoping I did not sound as overly eager as I felt.

"Tell me about you." Caleb settled back against the couch. "You said you work for the military base spinning stuff?"

"Yes." At least this was something I could answer easily. "I spin my webs for them. Different consistencies, different strengths."

"What do they do with it?"

I shrugged. "After they collect it, I have no idea. I think a lot of it is being analyzed for purposes of replicating it for use."

"What sorts of things can it be used for?" Caleb tipped his head, making his blond hair fall over one shoulder, and I had to resist the urge to reach out to brush it away.

"Many things. It is nearly unbreakable. I know they want to try using it in some military protective gear, and they mentioned that it might be used in hospitals too."

"I could see how that might be really useful. Is it really that strong though?" Caleb asked.

I gave of the webs a pluck to make it vibrate. "Yes."

"Could your web support me?"

"Quite easily. Would you like to try?"

He blinked in surprise, then nodded. "If that's okay."

"Of course," I said. It was awfully sweet of him to ask.

He glanced up at my tangle of webbing going on. "Um, how do I get up there?"

"Will I hurt you if I lift you?" I asked.

Caleb looked down at his scarred right side, then back up. "No, I don't think so. That won't hurt you?"

I giggled. If he only knew the size of some of the creatures I had lifted back in the monster world. "I'll be fine," I reassured him.

I wrapped two sets of my legs around him, being careful not to dig into his skin. I lifted him off the ground, and his arms reached out, his left catching me around the neck, his right forearm on my shoulder for balance. I moved with him, carrying him as easily as I carried a gallon of juice, backing myself up on my web until I was in the middle of it, between the first and second level of the open room, before lying him down on it. His left hand moved up to hold onto one of the strands, and I could see how tightly he clenched it, as though it was the only thing anchoring him in place. "You can let go," I said, drawing my legs carefully back. "You won't fall, I promise."

Caleb hesitated, and then his fingers slowly unwound from the webbing. Despite the 45-degree angle his body was at, he stayed perfectly in place, stuck securely to the strands. He shifted a bit, and the vibrations went through the web, sending a prey-drive instinct through me that I suppressed, though my mouth watered a bit automatically. "Wow. This is weird."

"I'm sure it is."

"I kinda feel like a fly," he said, then glanced at me and

frowned slightly. "Sorry, is that offensive?"

"No, I am not offended."

Caleb shifted again, running his fingers over the webbing. "It's so strong, and it's sticky, but it's not." He smiled. Even with his scarred lip, it still lit up his face. "This is kind of fun." I gave one of the threads a twang, and it made the whole weave shiver. Caleb grabbed for the webbing like he would fall, but he wasn't going anywhere easily or quickly. "That's so weird. So, you can feel the movement from anywhere?"

"Yes," I said. "If the threads are connected, I can feel the slightest vibration from a good distance away."

"And that's how you'd catch prey in the monster world?" Caleb asked.

"Yes."

"Huh." He shifted around again, glancing down at the webbing that supported him. "I almost feel like I'm floating. There's like no pressure on me anywhere."

"Is that a good thing?" I asked, slightly worried that it was making him nervous.

"Yeah. Really good," Caleb said, settling back onto the webbing. "There's no pressure on my scars. I feel like I could take a nap right here."

I smiled a bit. "You can if you want to."

"No, I'm not going to take a nap on our date," Caleb said with a grin. "Could you show me how you spin?"

"Yes, of course," I said, backing away from him. "I will redo this corner, it's getting dusty anyway." I slid one of my feet over the tight web strands, and they broke as easily as scissors through paper.

Caleb watched in surprise. "You said it's almost unbreakable."

"It is," I said, slicing through more strands and letting it fall to the ground. "But I can cut my own webbing, and most of that of other spiders."

Caleb chuckled. "I suppose something would have to be able to break it."

I nodded, starting a filament of webbing. My spinnerets moved to weave them together into the thickness I needed as I manipulated the fibers with my feet into a pattern in the corner. It was easy work, second nature to me. And, since I could watch television while I did, it made for quite a relaxing job and meant I got through a lot of human art.

Caleb sat up a little on my web, watching me as I carefully knitted the strands together, as neatly as I possibly could. Not that he would be able to tell if it was not perfect, but I would know, and I wanted to show him my best work. "You're so fast," he commented.

"I'm used to it," I said, giving him a grin.

"Could you wrap me up?" Caleb asked suddenly.

His words made me freeze. Something hot surged inside of me, and I had to swallow. Just imagining Caleb trapped in my webbing, struggling but unable to free himself, made me feel things deep inside of me that I could not name. I had pictured it before, not just with him, but with a human in general. Not a prey drive, exactly, but something in me that wanted to be powerful. Something that made me want to show my strength and that I was not as tiny as I had grown up believing. "I, um… I could," I said slowly.

Caleb cocked his head as he gazed at me. "But?"

I cleared my throat, sure my face was flushed. I quickly shook my head and returned my eyes to my spinning, even though I could have done it with all eight eyes closed.

"Come on, Ter, you can be honest with me," Caleb said, and I looked up in surprise at the shortening of my name. Caleb didn't even seem aware that he had done it.

"I am," I said, though I could hear the lie in my own voice and was unsurprised that Caleb did too.

"No, you're not. What is it? Did I say something wrong?"

I quickly shook my head again, lest Caleb think that he was the one having inappropriate thoughts. "No, you didn't."

"Why wouldn't you?" Caleb asked. "Cause I could damage your web?"

I couldn't stop a small hum of laughter. "You wouldn't."

"Would it make it so I can't breathe?" Caleb asked.

"It would depend on how you were wrapped up," I said.

"So then, why did you get so weird all of a sudden?"

"No reason."

"You're not good at lying, Ter. You won't hurt my feelings or anything. Why would you not wrap me up?"

My whole body burned with embarrassment, and all of

my movement stopped. "Because I don't want to be bad."

Caleb stared at me, not seeming to comprehend my words. The silence stretched between us for what felt like hours but was probably only a few seconds before he said, "Okay, you're going to have to explain that to me."

"Explain what?" I asked.

"Why would wrapping me up make you bad?" Caleb asked.

He had to be teasing me; it was so obvious. "Because that's what bad people do."

"I'm still not getting what you're saying," Caleb said, struggling to sit up from my web. I moved over to adjust the fibers with one of my feet so he could sit all the way up. "Thanks. What do you mean, that's what bad people do?"

"Don't you watch television?" I asked him.

"Of course, I do," he said.

Heat burned in my eyes, and I might have started crying if I had tear ducts. "On television, it's the bad people who tie people up. Or they get tied up because they're bad and need to be tied up."

Caleb blinked. "Ter, do you think that tying someone up makes you into a villain?"

I heard the tremor in my own voice as I said, "I've only seen it in movies, and usually the villain ties up the hero. Or the hero ties up the villain when he is captured. I don't want to be a villain. I want people to like me and not be afraid of me."

Caleb let out a very uninhibited laugh that startled me. "Teracht. You aren't a villain for thinking it's sexy to tie someone up. It's so common."

I frowned. "I know it happens a lot, but it's the bad guy doing it."

"Damn, okay, a lot to unpack here," Caleb said, rolling his eyes to the ceiling thoughtfully for a moment before looking back to me. "Tying someone up is a pretty normal fantasy for humans. And not because they are bad or villains or whatever. Some humans like to be tied up, and some humans like to tie them up, for fun."

I looked up to meet his eyes, sure my surprise was written all over my face. "For fun? Really?"

Caleb laughed. "Really! Fuck, there's a whole industry based around it."

"There is?" I asked, feeling more than a little foolish at my naiveté.

"Yes," Caleb said. "Bondage is all over porn."

"That is when humans are naked and pleasuring one another? I have not watched that sort of thing." I wondered if I was hot enough to just melt into a puddle of goo on the floor. Perhaps Caleb would think me unworthy of his attention if I could not even understand something as simple as human sexuality.

"Yeah. Or themselves, or... all kinds of things. I can show you if you want. Do you like just guys? Girls?"

I blinked. "I like you."

Caleb grinned. "Oh yeah?"

"Did I say something wrong?" I asked, worried that perhaps I had spoken out of turn.

"No," Caleb said. "No, it's fine. Is there sexual orientation in the monster world?"

"I don't know," I admitted. "For my species, we copulate with females to produce young."

"Humans do that too," Caleb said. "But not all... copulation is for breeding purposes. Humans do it because it's fun."

I hummed thoughtfully. "I suppose when you are not concerned about being eaten, copulation could be made pleasurable."

"Why do I feel like you mean that literally?" Caleb asked.

"Hmm? You mean, being eaten?" Caleb nodded. "Yes, I mean that literally. Obviously not all monsters eat one another, but with my kind, it is not unexpected that if one is too slow or too small, one could get eaten."

Caleb wrinkled his nose. "Well, that's not disturbing. But anyway, I'm going to assign you some homework before I come over again."

He was planning to return. That thought made me lighthearted. But home... work? "I already work from home," I said.

Caleb snorted with laughter. "Human term. When we go to school, we get homework, which is school stuff to do at home."

"Oh." That made very little sense to me, that school would also be done at home. But then, what did I really know about human education? "So, you are giving me school stuff to do?"

"Kind of," Caleb replied. "It's educational, at least. I'm going to send you some videos and some sites to look at. If you're comfortable with that, of course."

"Why would I not be?" I asked.

Caleb shrugged. "Not everyone is into porn. Well, most people are, but I'm sure there are a few who aren't. And stuff like that needs to be consensual."

I smiled a bit. "Human sex with consent is so different than with my species."

"Yeah, I'm getting that impression," Caleb said. "So, I'm going to send you some stuff this week, and then we can have this conversation again, okay?"

"Okay," I agreed. I didn't really know what to expect with what he would send me or what we would talk about after he did, but if Caleb kept coming back to spend time with me, I would talk about anything he wanted.

Chapter 7

Caleb

As soon as I got home Saturday evening, I started browsing online, assembling some links to send to Teracht. It was a little weird, going through porn sites looking for bondage porn that was not too over the top but still would give him an understanding about human desires and BDSM. I found a few sex-positive articles too, with some helpful tips. The list I sent him was not short, so I was surprised when I woke up on Sunday morning to a text from him.

TERACHT: Is there more?

I was assuming he meant more porn, and I wondered if I had just created a monster, figuratively speaking. I sent him links to more videos and some books online that maybe he could look at. I wasn't sure if he was much of a reader, but I figured it couldn't hurt.

Monday evening, Teracht sent some links back to me that I prayed were not viruses, but I opened them to find a variety of Not Safe For Work videos and images, and not the ones I had sent him. He had obviously found them on his own. He had some questions, which I thought was rather cute. He seemed much more confident asking me things via text than he did in person, but I supposed a lot of people were like that. I tried to answer everything I could from my own knowledge. I hadn't exactly been a slut in my sexual years. I had a few longer relationships, one of which lasted almost two years before we decided to call it quits, and I'd had a number of one-night stands and a handful of repeat partners at various times. I wasn't a prude, but I also was not exactly the most exciting person in bed either. I didn't go to sex clubs or swinger parties, though I had been dragged to a few in my earlier modeling days. It just wasn't my scene. I liked being photographed, sometimes even nude, but when it came to actual sexual activity, I preferred to keep that private.

He had more questions when he started sending me porn with women in it, but his interest still seemed to gravitate back toward guys. I considered myself pansexual; I could work with whatever someone had if I liked them, and I wasn't strictly dominant in bed either. A couple of my partners had tied me up once or twice, usually just with ribbon or something we had on hand, nothing overly elaborate. But I had to admit that Teracht's curiosity about the whole thing, as well as his concern about not being evil, intrigued me.

I wasn't sure how soon he wanted to get together, so I suggested Friday night, and he agreed. Every day leading up to that, he would send me more porn and ask more questions. Whatever government lackey got to review our communications probably was disgusted, or maybe turned on, who knows.

Friday afternoon, I found myself primping even more than I had for last week. I wasn't sure what to expect, but if Teracht wanted to start investigating his urges, I wanted to be ready. I had not replaced my car after the accident; I wasn't sure if I would ever get behind the wheel of a vehicle again. Most everything in Edgewind was within walking distance, and there was a bus that went around town, as well as a train that went to the surrounding areas. I often rode the bus if I was going across town; being in a confined space with a smaller number of people made me less self-conscious than walking down the street where I might run into any number of acquaintances. And, while it wasn't constant, sometimes my scars were overly sensitive to temperature, especially cold, and having my scarf tied so tight to keep out the chill physically hurt my face and neck. But the weather was starting to warm up, and I made the choice today to wear my scarf around my neck instead of wrapped around my face.

I stepped off the bus at the stop a short distance from Teracht's house. My phone pinged in my pocket with some sort of message, and I pulled it out as I moved away from the curb, checking to see if it was anything important, but it was just some marketing stuff.

A wolf whistle caught my attention, and I turned to see two large guys leaning against the wall of a nearby building. They were younger than me, probably students at the college, definitely jocks. One had his phone out and up, obviously taking a picture or maybe even filming me. "Dude, you got a dragon for a girlfriend?" the one not filming said. "She get too hot for you?"

The old me would have said something snappy and flirty in return. Something to let these punks know that I wasn't intimidated by their posturing and that they would be lucky to find someone like me who'd be willing to suck their dicks. But that was the old me. And the new me was intimidated as fuck. My hand immediately went to try to readjust my scarf to hide my face, but being flustered and with only one hand, I couldn't get it to move.

The one filming me smirked. "Smile for the camera, gorgeous."

I forced my feet to move, flipping them the bird with my left hand as I walked past them. I tried to keep my head up, feeling their eyes and their phone on me until I turned the corner. All I wanted to do was run, but I forced myself to walk at a steady pace until I reached Teracht's gate. He must have been watching for me, because he had the front door open by the time I was through the gate, holding it open for me to enter.

I stepped inside and realized as I pulled my jacket off that I was shaking. Teracht took my coat but paused when his hand brushed mine. "Caleb? What is it?"

I took a deep breath and shook my head. "Nothing."

Teracht frowned as he put my coat in the closet. "The way you said 'nothing' does not sound like nothing."

I toed off my shoes to avoid answering, then moved to sit on the couch. Teracht followed me at a slight distance. "Is something wrong?"

"No," I said, then looked up in surprise as Teracht slid his segmented body onto the couch to sit next to me instead of crawling up onto his web where he usually sat.

"Did I do something wrong?"

"No!" I said quickly, turning to him. "No, you're just fine. A couple of dickwads just harassed me on my way here."

Teracht's eyes narrowed, and for a moment, I saw the predator he once had been. He hissed, a sound that made every hair on my body stand up. "Did they hurt you?"

"I'm fine," I said, holding up my hand reassuringly. "They didn't touch me."

Teracht's eyes, all eight of them, were still slitted dangerously. "Do I need to report them to the police?"

"No," I said again, my chest warming at how much he wanted to help. "The police aren't going to do anything about a couple of catcalls. It's nothing I haven't dealt with before. I'm fine, really."

Teracht looked uncertain. "That doesn't seem right, that they should be able to do that."

I reached up my hand and placed it on his forearm, though I could see I was still shaking. "Yeah, I know."

Teracht shifted closer, and suddenly his arms and several pairs of his legs wrapped around me and pulled me close against him. I blinked at the sudden close contact but carefully wrapped my arms lightly around him. "Humans have a way of hurting one another with words," Teracht said, and I felt the rumble of his voice against me as I hugged him. "And while the wounds do not show, I think they can cut much deeper than physical ones can."

I let out a shaky breath. "Yeah," I admitted, curling closer to him. His skin was smooth but warm, and I realized that this was the longest he and I had ever held a single touch. In fact, it was the longest touch I had had since before my accident. I hadn't realized up until that moment how much I missed hugs. "It hurt, but I'm all right."

Teracht nodded solemnly, not letting me go yet. "It makes me sad that anyone would hurt you, Caleb."

I smiled softly. "Thanks. I appreciate that."

Teracht pulled back just enough so he could look down into my face, his hand sliding up to hold my cheek. "Are you all right?"

"Yes," I said, forcing myself to smile. I didn't like him

looking so concerned and upset. "I'm all right, Ter, I promise."

Teracht leaned down and kissed me gently. And, for a reason I could not pinpoint, something about that kiss broke me. I felt a lump in my throat that choked me as heat gathered behind my eyes, and suddenly I was crying. Teracht's arms around me tightened and held me close, and I couldn't stop. Deep, gasping sobs tore at me, and I felt the hot glide of tears over my cheeks and jaw. The fingers on my left hand curled tightly on Teracht's chest, pressing there like I wanted to absorb into him. My scarred cheek pressed to his shoulder, so smooth and gentle against my skin.

I couldn't say why I was crying then. I had shed a few tears here and there during my recovery, but I had not ever sobbed the way I was now. My brain was full of everything and nothing at the same time. I was angry, and lost, and in so much pain, and struggling with how I was supposed to feel. Taking the loneliness, the cruelty, and the shock of dealing with such a life-changing event, and then topping it with Teracht's genuine concern for my well-being hit me like a bolt of lightning, sending every emotion in my body into overdrive. I don't know how long we sat like that as I sobbed. I didn't think I had ever cried that hard in my life. Sobs that shook me and made me ache all over. Tears that made my cheeks tingle with a strange, hot numbness. I felt oddly aware of everything about myself, every bit of pain, every imperfection, every inch of intact skin that told a completely different story from the one I was living. But he just held still, the rise and fall of his chest the only movement as he held me in his embrace.

It was a long time before the tears stopped, and even longer before I finally pulled myself off of Teracht's chest, realizing my crying had left wet patches and trails down his skin. "S... Sorry," I said, trying hard not to snuffle as I scrubbed at my face with the back of my hand.

Teracht shook his head. He was gazing at me with all eight of his eyes half-lidded and gentle. "You don't have to apologize."

"I do. This is the second fucking time I've cried at your house, and I've only been here three times." My cheeks still tingled as I spoke, the corners of my mouth feeling stiff with saltiness.

"Caleb." My name in his voice was soft and soothing. "You do not have to worry about crying around me. It is only us here." Teracht's hand slid up to stroke over my cheek. "I will not ever judge you for crying."

That caused a few more tears to spill down my face. How could someone be so kind and yet so terrified of the world at the same time?

Teracht kissed me gently. "I'll be right back."

I nodded, and he got up, skittering away swiftly into the kitchen. I tried to straighten my hair and brush the tears off my face, then nearly lost it again when Teracht returned with a paper towel for me to blow my nose and a damp cloth to wipe my face. "God, thank you," I said, taking them gratefully.

Teracht nodded, waiting until I had put myself back into some semblance of order. "What else do you need?"

I exhaled softly. "Just you."

He blinked, then slid onto the couch. He adjusted around until he was stretched out on it, looking a little awkward, but then he held out his arms to me, and I curled into them. "Is this all right?"

"Yeah," I said.

"Do you have to go home tonight?" he asked.

"No."

"Then, stay with me?" It sounded like a question, the way his voice went up, and I nodded slowly.

"Okay." My heart gave a little skip in my chest as I realized he was asking me to stay over at his house. We weren't even sleeping together yet. That thought made me smile a little, but my sobbing had wrung me out to dry, and I was suddenly exhausted. "I might fall asleep here on you."

"I want you to."

I shifted to glanced up at Teracht. "You do?"

Teracht nodded and kissed my forehead. "You are comfortable, and I like touching you."

"I like touching you too," I said and curled closer into his embrace, feeling several of his willowy legs wrap lightly around me, keeping me close. As much as I didn't want to admit it, closing my eyes sounded great. I cuddled into his chest, and I was asleep within minutes.

It was dark outside when I woke up. I opened my eyes slowly, finding myself still curled in Teracht's arms on the couch.

"Are you awake?" he asked suddenly, and I jumped.

"Shit. Yeah, I'm awake." I pulled my phone out of my pocket to check the time. It was after 2am. "Sorry. I probably woke you too."

"I do not need to sleep as often as you," Teracht said as I sat up, trying to clear the fog from my head.

"So, you've just been holding me on the couch for hours?" I asked. He nodded. "Okay, that's not creepy," I said, giving him a teasing grin.

He looked confused. "Should I not have?"

"No, it's just fine," I reassured him, leaning in to give him a kiss. My mouth felt like cotton, and my face still felt salty from crying earlier. "I could use something to drink though."

"I'll get something for you," Teracht said, and I rose to my feet, making my way to the bathroom. I splashed water on my face and ran my fingers through my hair to try to smooth it a bit. Once I was presentable, I stepped out to find Teracht waiting for me with a bottle of Gatorade already open.

"Thanks," I said, taking a long swig.

Teracht nodded, and I noticed he had a bottle of his own

too, with a straw in it. For some reason, seeing the straw made me smile as I moved back over to the couch and sat. "So, how often do you have to sleep?"

Teracht looked thoughtful. "Actual sleep, only an hour or two at most each day, and I can do it in short naps. But I rest a lot too. If I wove a web and waited for prey to come, I would sort of doze."

He really was like a housecat, I thought as I drank my beverage. Outside, there was a faint light from the moon and the nearby streetlight filtering through the curtains, but the room was still fairly bright from the few lamps and overhead lights, casting strange shadows from the webs strung everywhere. He had once more settled onto his web a little above me, sucking contentedly at his own drink. "I suppose you get through a lot of TV that way too."

He nodded. "I do. Though I have not watched as much this week."

"Oh, why not?" I asked.

"I was looking at the videos and things you sent me," Teracht replied, and I flushed, remembering the amount of porn we had sent back and forth that week.

"Oh."

"It was all very informative," Teracht added. "I learned a lot. Thank you for giving me homework."

"Uh, you're welcome. I'm glad you found it interesting."

"Do you need to go back to sleep?" Teracht asked as I finished my Gatorade and set the bottle aside.

"No, I'm good for now," I said. That had been almost a full night's sleep just based on when I got to Teracht's house and when I fell asleep. Now that I was hydrated, I was feeling pretty awake. "How about you?"

"I'm all right," Teracht replied, smiling before setting his own empty bottle aside as well. He rested his chin on his folded humanoid arms, gazing down at me.

"Okay. Well, um…" I felt a blush rise in my cheeks. "Did the stuff I sent you inspire anything?"

Teracht looked surprisingly thoughtful. "I see now why you say that humans like being tied up."

"And not by bad people," I added.

"Yes." He focused his eyes on me. "Do you like being tied up?"

There was the question I had been waiting for. "To be honest, I don't know. I've done some pretty simple stuff. You know, sexy blindfolds, furry handcuffs, that sort of thing. I haven't gone full bondage with anyone."

"Oh," Teracht said softly, and I realized from the tone of his voice that he was afraid I was rejecting the idea.

"I'm open to it," I added quickly. "No reason to not give it a try, at least."

"You… you're willing to allow me to tie you up?" Teracht sounded much more eager than he had a few moments ago. That lifted my spirits. My little spider monster who had been so afraid of being a villain was all right with bondage now that he had watched a whole bunch of human pornography and had a willing participant.

"Yeah," I said, then glanced down at my missing arm. "I mean, we might have to get a little creative."

Teracht nodded. "That is simple. My webbing won't slip if I use the right kind."

I brought my forearms together experimentally, trying to imagine them wrapped up with spider webs. "Fair enough. Um..." I licked my lips as I met his dark eyes again. "Did you only want to tie me up?"

Teracht tilted his head to study me. "Are you asking if I would like to put my penis inside of you too?"

Wow, that was a lot more straight-forward than I had heard it put before, but I nodded slowly. "Yeah, something like that. Or, did you have other ideas?" The idea of being tied up in Teracht's web and potentially fucked by his monster dick that I had yet to see sent a weird thrill through my body.

Teracht's cheeks blushed extremely dark. "I..."

"What?" I prompted.

He bit his lower lip as he tried to put into words something that he didn't seem certain about. "I don't... think that I am meant to experience sexual pleasure."

I blinked. "Uh, okay, why do you think that?"

Teracht frowned. "The things you sent me. The humans were obviously feeling a lot of pleasure. And the human males, it's obvious when they are aroused."

"Yeah," I said, curious where he was going with that.

"My anatomy does not do that," Teracht said, the blush seeming to spread through his whole body. "Even if I touch myself like humans do, there is no distinct pleasure from it."

I thought about that for a minute. I supposed it would make sense that when you were at risk of being killed while trying to mate, the focus was not on pleasure, but rather, staying alive and trying to do it as fast as possible. And just because here he didn't have to worry about me killing him in the middle of sex didn't mean that his anatomy and bodily responses changed. Also, that was weird, thinking about spiders masturbating. "It might just not be your thing," I offered, wondering if he might have changed his mind about the whole thing if he couldn't get sexual pleasure from the experience.

He looked sadly at me. "But I want you to like it."

"Well, we're getting a little ahead of ourselves anyway," I said. "I don't even know if I'll like being tied up. Why don't we try it and then go from there?"

Teracht blinked all eight eyes, then smiled brightly. "Yes. That is very smart, Caleb."

"Aww." I gave him a sheepish grin. "Thanks, Ter. So, what's our safe word going to be?"

"Safe... word?" Teracht said. "Oh, yes. What you say if you want to stop?"

I nodded. "Or if you do, not just me."

That thought had obviously not occurred to him by the look that came over his face, but then Teracht nodded. "That makes sense. What should be our safe word?"

I glanced around the room. "Gatorade," I said, nodding at the two empty bottles sitting nearby. Easy for both of us to remember.

Teracht giggled, legit *giggled*, at that. "Okay," he agreed. "How do we do this?"

I hesitated. Not like I wanted to top from the bottom, as it were, but I was sure I had more sexual experience than Teracht did, no matter how much porn he watched this last week. "Well, um... Do you want me to be naked?"

Teracht blushed. Despite the fact that he had seen me naked before, this was obviously a much different scenario. "What are you comfortable with?"

"Um, whatever." Okay, I was not helping. And I had no idea how far this little experiment was going to go. "How about I keep my underwear on for now? If I don't like something, I'll let you know?"

Teracht nodded slowly. "Yes, that seems reasonable."

"Okay." I gave him a small smile. He was so shy about it, but that didn't seem to be what he wanted. He wanted to be in charge, he just wasn't sure how to do it. I didn't want to control what he did too much, but I could at least get the game started. "Then give me an order, sir."

Chapter 8

Teracht

CALEB SUDDENLY CALLING ME 'sir' sent heat through my body in a way that reminded me of when I sensed prey approaching, about to stumble into my web. I felt my jaw almost hit the floor as I stared at him, a small smirk playing over his lips. I couldn't stop myself from leaning in, catching his face in my hands, and kissing him firmly. His left hand came up to hold onto mine. I stroked my thumb over his right cheek, feeling the twisted skin beneath it. He was doing this for me. He was trusting me. I couldn't let him down.

I pulled back from the kiss to gaze at him. His face was slightly flushed, his hair a little messy where my hands had caught it. Hair I had stroked while he slept on the couch next to me so I would always have the memory of it, in case he changed his mind and decided not to have anything more to do with me. "Take your clothes off." The words felt strange in my mouth, and I knew that it sounded more like a request than an order. But it was my first one. It would take time for me to find that voice.

Caleb grinned and stepped back from me, grabbing his shirt and maneuvering it over his head, tossing it onto the couch, followed by the undershirt. He reached for his pants and slid them down and off, then sat on the edge of the couch to remove his socks, leaving him in just his red boxer briefs. He stood up and resumed his spot in front of me, waiting for my next order, and I realized I had no idea what to say or do. I had spent this past week watching videos of every variety of porn I could find. But porn looked different than the romance of movies, and neither of them were honest. It was all acting, that much I knew. Was Caleb acting for me now? Was I acting for him? What did I want from him?

"Turn around," I said after a moment. Caleb blinked, but he shifted a half turn on his feet so his back was to me. I moved up behind him and saw goosebumps break out on his neck and shoulders. I had seen those gorgeous shoulders before, when we had done our exploring last week, but that had been educational. Practical. Clinical. Now he was nearly naked in my living room, doing what I told him to do. I leaned in and cautiously pressed my lips to the back of his left shoulder. He jumped and inhaled but did not pull away. His skin prickled again, and I slowly pressed kisses down the length of his spine until I reached his waistband. He shifted a little, but it wasn't to move away. Perhaps my human was ticklish. I hesitated before darting just the tip of my pointed tongue out to dip into the crease at the base of his spine. Caleb jumped again, but he didn't pull back. "Is that all right?" I asked.

"Yes," he said, his voice barely above a whisper.

I smiled and repeated the brush of my tongue before kissing my way back up his spine. My final kiss was pressed to his right shoulder, where the burned skin puckered together. I hesitated just a moment before giving his shoulder a light nip. I had no teeth, just the hard palate, and I made sure to keep it gentle. Caleb let out a soft exhale, and I felt his whole body relax under me. He had been so tense, and I hadn't realized it. Maybe if I could surprise him, he would relax further. "Do you trust me?" I asked in his ear.

"Yeah," Caleb said, his voice surprisingly soft.

That was good enough for me. I wrapped my arms and several sets of my legs around him, lifting him almost effortlessly off the ground, and tossed him. He let out a yelp as he flew through the air, a flail of arms and legs, and landed safely on my web, the strands moving only enough to absorb his speed and return to their place, as if I had tossed him onto a mattress. He let out a gasp of breath as he sprawled there, on his back. In another instant, I was over him, pinning him down with the bulk of my abdomen. "All right?"

"Fuck... Yeah." The words came out a little strangled, and

I could hear his heart pounding in his chest, but his eyes did not hold fear as he gazed up at me. "God, you're strong."

I beamed. He seemed to like that about me. I liked it too. "I am," I said, dropping my voice to what I hoped was a seductive purr, though I had little experience speaking that way. I grabbed his left arm and stretched it out. Before he could make any other movements, I began to quickly spin, weaving my web around his wrist until an almost solid cuff of white, gossamer spider silk held his arm in place. He watched it with fascination; I could feel the nervous tension in his body again, but I did my best to make sure I worked quickly and carefully. "You won't be able to break that," I said, giving the thread connecting it a twang, the reverberation going through the web, myself, and him. "You'll only be freed when I let you go. Or if you safe word," I added hastily, giving him a reassuring smile. The last thing I wanted to do right now was scare him. Well, maybe scare him in a good way. Was there a sexy way to scare someone? If there was, that was what I wanted. I wanted him to feel the power I had over him, to know that he was helpless in my web, trapped, my prey, my plaything, unless I felt like letting him go. And I didn't want to. Just seeing his one wrist bound to my web sent a heat through me that I had not known before.

Caleb gave a cursory struggle. I watched his arm muscles flex as he shifted and tugged at the restraint, but I was right. He wasn't going anywhere. He turned his eyes back to me. I smiled hopefully. "Is that all right?"

"Yes," he said.

A little disappointment lurched in me. I had to be confident and speak up and tell him what I wanted. He had told me he wanted me to be honest. He was trusting me, so I had to do the same in return. "Yes, what?" I prompted.

He blinked in confusion for a moment. "Yes, sir?" he asked, making it question.

I pressed my mouth to his in a rewarding kiss, and he returned it, his right forearm resting on the spot where my neck connected to my shoulder, like he would hold my hair if he could. I was pressed up against him, and I realized as I shifted above him that he was hard underneath the fabric of his underwear, a small spot of wet already forming there. I had never been the object of someone's sexual desire before, and that felt strange, but also amazing.

I pulled back to study him. He wouldn't slide on my web, and his left arm was anchored in place. And I had no idea what to do next. Here he was, trapped, at my mercy, and my own inexperience was showing. "Um... wh... what do you want me to do?" I asked, sure my voice was a little shaky.

"Uh..." Caleb glanced around too, his cheeks a little pink. "What do you want to do?"

"I don't know," I admitted.

Caleb hesitated for a moment. "Why don't you wrap me up with webbing? So I can see what it's like."

I let out a breath and nodded. That seemed logical and also

pretty safe. I was used to wrapping prey up tightly with the intent of preventing it from escaping so I could feed. I wasn't going to wrap him like that; I'd suffocate him that way. "All right. Tell me if something is too tight."

"Do you have to spin me to wrap me up?" he asked.

I blinked, then realized that when I had demonstrated my capture technique to him with the juice bottle, I had spun the bottle dizzyingly fast to wrap it. Mostly that was to disorient the prey so it couldn't fight anyway. I doubted his human body would be able to handle that sort of speed and force, and he seemed to realize it too. "No!" I said, a little louder than I meant to, and I dropped my voice down again when Caleb jumped slightly. "No. Not at all. I can wrap you up in any number of ways just by using my legs to guide the webbing. And I can do it as fast or as slow as you want."

He nodded, watching me as I slid down and positioned myself by his bare feet. I ran one of my feet up the underside of his sole, and he jerked. Ah, another ticklish spot. I made a mental note of that before beginning to spin. My legs moved to help wrap around Caleb, passing the webbing around him and through the fibers of the web he was lying on. In almost no time, I had his right leg covered up to the hip in webbing, not too sticky, but enough that he wouldn't be able to move it.

"You're really fast," he commented as I switched to the other side, already halfway up his leg to his knee.

"Thank you," I said without looking up from what I was

doing to ensure I did not hurt him. "Is that too tight?"

"No," he said, trying to give his legs an experimental pull that I felt along the webbing, but they may as well have been encased in stone. "I really am stuck though."

"Yes, you are," I said before sliding up him a little. With his legs spread like that, his cock jutted inside of his underwear. He looked beautiful. I knew he didn't think it of himself anymore, but to me, the twisted, discolored skin was interesting and different, and it was hardly the worst injury I had ever seen after living in the monster world.

I bypassed his groin and began to weave just above his hips, wrapping him up so he couldn't move his chest except to breathe. "All right?" I asked him. "Take a few breaths for me."

He nodded slowly and did as I asked. I gave him a soft kiss on the lips before returning to my spinning, using my feet to pull and weave the web up by his throat, lightly pinning his head in place, threading carefully so as not to catch his gorgeous hair. I felt him swallow against the webbing at his throat. "Still breathing okay?"

"Yeah," he said, letting out a soft exhale. I began to loop my webbing around his shortened right arm. This was the one area I was concerned about, as most of Caleb's injuries were focused on his right arm, shoulder, and neck, as well as his missing hand. I did not want to wrap him too tightly, in case the skin was extra sensitized, but I also did not want him to be able to move so as not to rub his damaged skin on my web, which I thought might be just as unpleasant as squeezing. Caleb watched me, his blue eyes wide and solemn, until I reached where his forearm abruptly ended, curling a few more strands around it to keep the whole thing pinned to my web.

I finally turned back to him. Only his left arm, face, and groin area were free of my webbing, and there was a slight tremble in his left hand that made me worried. I reached up and tangled my fingers with his, giving them a light squeeze. "Are you all right? Are you hurting anywhere?"

Caleb tried to shake his head, but my webbing kept him from being able to move his head much. "No, it just feels weird," he admitted. "But good. I think I like it. It doesn't hurt anywhere."

I nodded, stroking several of my feet over his wrapped right side. "It is not bothering your skin here?"

"No," he said, sounding a little surprised. "Not at all. The bandages I had to wear were more irritating than this. This feels... 'Good' maybe isn't the right word. Secure?"

I smiled. He was definitely secure. "As long as I'm not hurting you," I said, giving him another sweet kiss. He whimpered when I pulled away, though I don't think he meant to.

"What do you think?" he asked, rolling his eyes down to indicate his enmeshed form. "Do you like this?"

My mouth was watering a little as I followed his gaze down his body. "I do," I said. "You're beautiful."

He blushed, and I felt his left arm pull, like he wanted to try to cover his face, but it wasn't getting out of the webbing that manacled him. "I'm not."

"Yes, you are." I realized with a spark of delight that he couldn't move his arms or his head to cover his face. I reached up my hand to stroke it over his right cheek. "You're perfect, and beautiful, and amazing, and you need to know that and hear it all the time."

Caleb bit his lip, trying to shake his head. "Teracht-"

"Mm. Maybe I'll just leave you tied up here until you believe me," I said lightly. Not that I had any intention of doing that, but I thought it sounded good. He must have thought so too, because his uncovered hips gave a small jerk. I grinned and slid down his frame to where his cock gave a pulse under the red fabric. The wet patch there was growing, and I ran my thumb over it curiously. He sucked in a breath. He felt hot and silky through the material. I glanced up at him, rubbing my thumb over the spot again. "You like that?"

"Yeah." The word was only an exhalation of breath.

I hadn't intended for this to turn into anything sexual, but Caleb tangled in my web, his cock straining the fabric, was absolutely gorgeous, and I wanted to watch him squirm. I leaned in and placed my mouth a bit hesitantly over the bulge of cotton, letting my breath warm it. He let out a whine.

I stroked my fingers over it again. "May I?" I asked, motioning with my head to his need.

Caleb let out a soft moan. "Yes," he said, his voice husky.

I reached in and pulled his cock out through the slit of his boxer briefs. The head of his dick glistened with fluid, and it gave a pulse in my hand eagerly. The skin was so soft, and I traced my fingers carefully over it. Caleb moaned, his hips giving a little thrust, the only movement he could make. The vibrations went through my web, and heat surged inside of me once more. "Teracht..."

"Yes?" I purred, stroking my fingers over the head of his cock, getting the stickiness between my fingers.

"Touch me," he pleaded.

I laughed, stroking my fingers over the head again. "I will, pet, I will," I said. His eyes went wide at the sudden nickname, and I couldn't stop a giggle. "You like that?"

"Yeah," he said, his tongue catching his lower lip.

"What was that?" I prompted, removing my hand from his straining dick.

Caleb groaned and closed his eyes. "Yes, sir," he said.

"Yes, sir, what?" I said, wrapping my hand around his shaft and giving it a very light squeeze, not sure of my own strength or the delicateness of his human flesh. It seemed that he liked it though, because his moan got louder.

"What?" he asked, swallowing hard.

I grinned, sliding up his body so we were pressed together. I felt his cock push against the stiff hair of my abdomen, and he gasped at the sensation. "Do you like it when I call you 'pet?'"

Caleb groaned and tried to nod but couldn't, so he forced

out, "Yes, sir."

"Yes, sir, what?" I prompted again, letting one of my feet brush the underside of his dick. He gasped at the sensation, and I wondered how strange that was for him. "Tell me what you like."

He took a deep breath, causing the web to quiver, and said, "Yes, sir, I like it when you call me 'pet.'"

I nearly danced for joy at his words, but instead I rewarded him with an eager kiss, sliding my hand down his body to grasp his shaft a little tighter than before and give it a firm stroke. He moaned into my mouth, making me shiver, and I reached up to grab the top of his hair with my other hand, tipping his head back so I could thrust my tongue into his mouth. He let out a strangled "mmrf" sound, but his tongue tangled eagerly with mine. I was finding that kissing him and stroking him was taking a lot of coordination on my part. Luckily, I was used to multi-tasking. I stroked my hand up and down his shaft as my tongue battled his own, his teeth grinding on my lips. He whined, squirming against the ties that bound him, and the motion of the webbing was like music going through my body, his muscles pulsing and causing my webs to vibrate in such a glorious way that it made my body heat all over and warm me like I was lying in the sun.

He gave a sharp thrust of his hips into my touch with a cry against my mouth, and my hand and abdomen were suddenly covered in sticky fluid. I pulled back in surprise, glancing down to see the result of what I had wrought from him. I had watched plenty of porn this last week, with men orgasming into their own hands, onto the faces or chests or backs of others, but seeing it here now, instead of impersonally through a screen, was fascinating. I lifted the hand to my mouth, flicking out my tongue to taste his release curiously. Salty and thick, it was unlike anything I had experienced before. I spread my fingers, watching the sticky juices stretch between them like tiny webs.

Caleb was still breathing deeply, each one causing my web to shiver. His eyes were closed, his head tipped back where I still held him by the hair. I released my hold on it, letting the silky, gold strands melt through my fingers. He relaxed back with a sigh, his eyes peeking open to reveal a sliver of blue.

"All right?" I asked.

"Yeah," he said, voice low and husky.

"Good." I laid my hand on his chest, feeling the rise and fall of it beneath the cocoon. "But I didn't give you permission to orgasm."

He blinked, and then the most adorable red blush spread across his face. "I'm sorry, sir, you're right."

I smirked, kissing the corner of his mouth. "I'll forgive it this one time, we're both still learning."

"Thank you, sir," he said.

"I will leave you here to think about that," I said with a grin that I hoped made me look delightfully wicked. I would have to try that in the mirror. "I'll be back."

He whimpered softly, but he had to stay where he was, stretched out on my webbing, his dick softening. I left him there, giving the web a light twang as I climbed it so the vibrations would go through his sensitized body. He whined, and I smirked to myself. I went to the kitchen and washed my hands, then poured a glass of juice for myself, drinking it all, before I poured one for Caleb and put a straw in it, taking it back to him. "Drink, pet," I ordered him, holding the straw to his lips, and he took it into his mouth, drinking slowly and obediently until the entire glass was gone.

I kissed him softly again. "You are going to sleep now."

He blinked, looking like he wanted to protest, but I held up a finger to his lips to silence him. "It's still the middle of the night. And I'm not letting you down. You stay here and sleep like a good pet."

Caleb smiled softly. "Yes, sir," he said, his voice meek.

I shifted to cut a few of the lines holding the web so it swung down like a hammock, swaying gently back and forth with him, like a baby in a cradle. I watched him close his eyes. I knew it would probably take him a while to fall asleep now, but I was patient. After a long time, his breathing evened out into the deep breaths that indicated sleep. I smiled to myself as I picked up my phone to do some browsing online.

Chapter 9

Caleb

THE FIRST THING I realized when I woke up was that I couldn't move. I sucked in a panicked breath, giving a jerk, but my body would not respond to my commands. I forced my eyes open. The outside was lighter through the curtains now. Webby curtains. I stilled as I realized where I was and why I couldn't move.

The next moment, Teracht was next to me. "Are you all right, Caleb?"

"Yeah," I said, trying to blow a piece of hair off my face. Teracht brushed it away with his fingers. "I just forgot where I was."

Teracht nodded. "Did you sleep well?"

"Yeah," I said, realizing I felt pretty good. "What time is it?"

"A little after seven," he said.

I sighed, then jumped as he reached out one of his spider legs and ran it along the webbing that bound my left leg to the web. It split underneath his touch like skin under a surgeon's scalpel, and I reminded myself once more that I was glad I was not seen as prey by him. He cut loose all of the bonds that held me, then helped me to sit up, the web swaying a little beneath our weight but not breaking.

"Thank you for last night," I said as I stretched. "It was great."

"Were you happy?" he asked, looking hopeful.

"Very," I said. "Your webs are a little weird. I admit I had a few flashbacks to when I was in the hospital on the burn unit and couldn't move much."

Teracht's face fell just a bit. "I'm sorry."

"No," I said, putting out my hand to touch his forearm in reassurance. "It's all right, really."

"I don't want you to be afraid, Caleb."

"I wasn't afraid," I assured him, reaching up to touch his cheek. "I promise, Ter. I knew you were there and that I was safe."

He turned his head to kiss my palm lightly. "You are safe with me, always, Caleb."

"Thank you." I stroked his cheek again.

He smiled softly, but there was a sadness behind it that tugged at my heart. "Do you have to leave now?"

I blinked. "It's Saturday, right?" He nodded. "Do you

have to work?"

He shook his head. "No. But even if I did, I could spin while still talking to you."

I nodded. "I don't have anywhere I have to be today. Or, ever, really. My next physical therapy appointment isn't until Tuesday, and I don't have anything planned until then."

He perked up a little. "You could stay?"

"Yeah. If you want me to."

He nodded eagerly, then frowned a bit. "I'm afraid I don't have much in the way of food, only liquids."

I shrugged. "Hey, that's what grocery delivery is for."

Teracht beamed. "I do have everything delivered anyway."

I nodded. "I should clean up, but I'll do an online order and get some stuff. Food, maybe a couple toiletries." I wanted to brush my teeth. "If that's cool with you."

"Yes, of course!" he said eagerly, and I laughed.

"Awesome. Can I use your shower?"

Teracht nodded, motioning up the stairs to the second floor. "Yes."

"Is that the only thing up there that you use?" I asked curiously, realizing that I had never seen him go into any of that area while I had been here.

"Pretty much. There are two bedrooms, but I sleep on my web down here, so they are open."

All this space, and he lived by himself. That must have been lonely. "Okay. Is there a place I can charge my phone? My charging cord is in my jacket pocket."

He nodded. "I'll get it for you," he offered, then suddenly reached down to slide me off the web that had kept me perfectly in place for hours. He set me on the ground like a parent lowering a baby who was learning to walk. "Thanks." He nodded, moving over to grab my charger as I gathered my clothes. "I'll order some breakfast, and then I'll order some groceries and stuff. Do you want anything?"

He placed the cord on top of my clothing pile. "No, I am fine."

"Okay," I said, then headed upstairs. It was a little slow going, as the stairs, wall, and banister were covered with an intricate pattern of webbing. It wasn't slippery, but the texture was still new to me, and despite his reassurances, I was still concerned I might break the webbing he worked so hard to create. Teracht pointed to the left. "In the middle there."

"Thanks. I'll be down in a bit," I said, and he nodded.

I closed myself in the bathroom, figuring ordering breakfast would be my first priority. I was actually planning to stay at Teracht's house all weekend? The idea had crossed my mind, but I honestly had thought that our date last night would have turned into a "Netflix and chill" situation, and then I would go home again, or leave in the morning. But it wasn't like I had anything there that needed my attention. Hell, I didn't even have a plant or a fish to worry about keeping alive.

I placed a delivery order with the nearest restaurant that

was open, and I added on a chocolate milkshake for Teracht as well. Maybe he'd like it. I made sure to tip extra well for the early-morning delivery. Then I turned on the shower. I stepped in, realizing that there was no shampoo or soap, so I just scrubbed as best I could. And of course, it was only after that I realized there also was no towel. Drip dry it was then. I didn't want to slip on the bathroom floor, so I grabbed my phone that I had left to charge on the counter and began to add some things from the local store to a cart. A towel set, toothbrush and toothpaste, a comb, deodorant, a pack of underwear and undershirts, some soap and shampoo, toilet paper. Then I started adding groceries. Nothing too crazy, and not too much, since I wasn't sure I was going to be here the whole weekend. It wasn't like I was moving in or anything. I made sure to change the delivery address to Teracht's house, and again, I added an extra-large tip.

Once I was sure I wasn't going to die on the tile floor, I climbed out of the shower, using my undershirt as a makeshift towel to wipe away remaining wetness. I got dressed, rinsed my mouth, ran my fingers through my hair, and checked myself in the large mirror in front of the sink. Caleb Webster the fashion model looked back at me from one side of my face. The other side I still didn't recognize after all of this time. The twisted, discolored skin on my face and neck, the way my empty right sleeve dangled down at an odd angle after my elbow. When I looked at myself, it was still all I could see. Was that what Teracht saw too? He told me he had seen my pictures online, but he had never once made a comment about how different I looked with my injured face and body. What did he see in me? Half a pretty face? Someone who was damaged goods? I had no idea.

The sound of the doorbell startled me, and I realized that breakfast must have arrived. I headed out of the bathroom and down the stairs to find Teracht hovering nervously by the window. "I got it," I said, moving over to the front door. I unlocked the deadbolt and pulled the door open. The delivery driver had obviously given up on waiting for the food to be picked up, having left the bag and a tray with two beverages in front of the door. He was getting into his car to drive off, and I caught the moment he saw me when I opened the door. Fear. I scared him. My heart sank a little as I grabbed the plastic bag, holding it out to Teracht to take before I picked up the beverage tray, balancing it carefully with my one hand. I pushed the door shut with my forearm, and Teracht leaned over to lock it. It had been so long since I had answered a door like that, and I suddenly realized why Teracht had everything delivered and did not go to the military base to spin his webs. The world outside that door was full of people who were afraid. People who were angry. People who were disgusted. Of ugliness, of monsters, of those different than themselves. People who didn't understand what it was like to be different and didn't care.

I moved into his open kitchen, deciding that standing to

eat at the center island would work fine. I hadn't been in his kitchen yet, and I realized with a start that he actually had two refrigerators and no oven or stovetop. I supposed that made sense if all of his food was liquid. Teracht joined me on the other side of the island, lining up several different bottles of juice. I pulled the milkshake from the tray, adding it to the end of the line. He glanced up at me curiously. "What is that?"

"Chocolate milkshake," I said, opening the plastic lid to show him. "It's basically just milk and ice cream blended together, but it's liquid, there's nothing solid in it."

Teracht gave me a shy smile. "I am excited to try it."

"Good." I pulled out my Styrofoam container of pancakes and sausage, glad to see that they had included a plastic fork and knife with it as well as some packets of maple syrup. I suspected that Teracht did not have silverware either.

Teracht watched me cut my pancakes. I offered him a bite, as they were quite soft, but he declined. But he picked up the milkshake, having to put some effort into the straw to draw the thicker part up, but he swallowed it, and all eight of his eyes lit up in delight. "That is oddly delicious," he said.

I swelled with pride at having introduced him to something new. He finished the entire milkshake in several large swallows, which I'm pretty sure would have made me sick or at least given me an ice cream headache if I drank it that fast, before he reluctantly set aside the empty cup and turned to the other bottles he had lined up. If I drank that much liquid in a day, I was sure I would never leave the bathroom, but he drank it all down easily as I ate my own breakfast. I was used to eating with my left hand now, at least, though it still was a little slow at times. He finished his beverages long before I had cleaned my plate.

"May I ask you a question?" he said after putting the empty bottles into his recycling bin that was already almost entirely full.

"Shoot," I said, waving my fork for him to ask while I continued to eat. I grabbed my coffee from the beverage tray and opened it, dumping in two containers of that shitty creamer stuff that restaurants used before closing it again.

"What we did last night," Teracht began slowly, and my stomach soured for a moment. Did he regret what we had done? Did he not enjoy it? Had he realized that tying me up wasn't as interesting as he thought it would be? I waited for him to continue. "I pleasured you, yes?"

I tried not to laugh. He looked so sincere. "Yes, you did," I said, taking a sip of my mediocre coffee.

He smiled a bit, then cleared his throat. "I, um... I enjoyed it too."

"Good!" I said. He shuffled his feet a little, which was strange to watch with his eight legs on the ground. "What is it?"

He picked up his phone, turning it toward me so I could see. It was a still shot of a naked young man bent over at the waist, leaning his forearms on the bed beneath him, a look of ecstasy on his face. Behind him, another naked man with a big bushy beard and a bald head had his dick buried deep inside of the younger guy's ass. I recognized it from one of the many links we had passed back and forth this last week. "Is this what you want me to do to you?"

I almost choked on my coffee, setting it down and clapping a paper napkin to my mouth as I swallowed. He stared at me, unblinking, still holding his phone for me to see. I coughed and cleared my throat. "Um..." He looked back at me, his eyes a little sad. I didn't like that. "Is that really your question?"

"Well, yes," he said, setting the phone down and staring at the image. "I mean, not entirely."

"Just say what you want to say, Ter," I said, taking another sip of coffee and then putting it aside so I didn't accidentally drown myself if he said something that surprised me. "I won't be mad or offended or anything, I promise."

"Okay." He took a deep breath and looked up at me. "In a lot of the porn I watched, the male inserts his penis into an orifice." I didn't think I'd ever heard a less sexy description of porn, but I just nodded. "And it seems like the person being penetrated enjoys it."

"Yeah?" Where was he going with this?

"I would like to bring you such pleasure," he said, his eyes meeting mine. "But I do not believe our anatomy is compatible."

"Well, um, I still haven't seen what you're working with,"

I ventured.

Teracht's cheeks went dark. "I could show you if you wanted."

"Yeah," I said. "If you're all right with it. If it's not going to work, then we'll figure something out. Just let me finish my coffee first."

Teracht nodded, scooping up his recycling bin and heading for the back door of the house to take it out. I wondered if that was the only time he ever went outside, to put out his trash and recycling and to pick up his items that he ordered.

I finished my drink by the time he came back in with the empty bin and set it back into place, and he washed his hands thoroughly like a human would. At least he was conscious of being clean. He nodded toward the living room and headed that way. I tossed my trash into the smaller can, washed my own hand and rinsed my mouth, then followed him to the living room.

Teracht was perched on his web lazily, gazing down at me with a small, shy smile. "Thank you again for the chocolate milkshake."

I nodded. "No problem. Glad you liked it. There are lots of other flavors we can try if you want."

He nodded eagerly. "I would like that."

"I'll keep that in mind," I said. "So... how do we... I... Uh..."

Teracht giggled softly, but the sound was more nervous

than cheerful. "I suppose it would be polite to ask first if I may show you... what I have."

"Oh. Yeah, sure, it's fine," I said, appreciating the creature not from this world being so concerned about consent. He was more polite than a few of the guys I had gone home with in my life.

Teracht nodded, then shifted a little on his web to roll onto his side, exposing his underbelly to me. It was not much different than the top of him, with the soft hair covering most of it, his spider legs attaching to his middle abdomen. On his larger back end, a small opening I had not seen before suddenly appeared, and out of it came what I could only think of as a ball. Perfectly round and somewhat smooth, I would guess it was a little bigger around than a ball gag. It protruded from his opening on what seemed to be a rather flimsy almost stick-like thing. The description that popped into my mind immediately was a cake pop, though that felt like a very weird way to think about the spider junk in front of me. It was very girthy, and my ass tightened a little at the idea of trying to take that inside me. I thought maybe it would be sort of like those knots that some of those weird wolf-shifter romances had, but just the whole thing as one large knot.

"Can I touch?" I asked, holding up my hand.

Teracht nodded. "Yes."

On his web as he was, his junk was almost at face level with me, so I reached out and carefully brushed it with my fingertips. It was a little spongy. Cake pop was definitely becoming the leading descriptor in my mind, and I was never going to be able to look at one again without laughing. I stroked it gently, then cupped my hand around it. "Does this feel good?"

Teracht suddenly looked sad. "No," he said.

"Sorry," I said, quickly pulling my hand back, and he shook his head.

"You're not hurting me, Caleb. It just doesn't feel any different than you touching me anywhere else."

I frowned a bit. That was kind of depressing, that he wasn't getting any sort of pleasurable sensation from his dick. "How exactly does atauri sex work again?"

"A male would subdue a female, usually by wrapping her up in his webbing, and then would inseminate her while she was freeing herself. He would insert this into her orifice, and then it would break off. There is sperm inside of the bulb, and it gets absorbed into the female's body to produce young."

"Doesn't that hurt you?" I asked.

Teracht shook his head, pointing to the thin stick-like base. "This has almost no sensation in it."

I ran my fingers gently over it, giving it a few experimental strokes and other movements, and Teracht watched all of them without any change to his body language or face. I had gotten more of a reaction from him the first time I had touched his chest than when I played with his dick. His frequent concerns about consent suddenly made a whole lot more sense to me too when I realized how non-consensual spider sex seemed to be. "So, if you lose your dick when you mate, does that mean you only mate once in your life?"

Teracht nodded. "Yes. And then we usually get eaten."

"What do you mean?"

"The females are much bigger than the males, so after the male deposits his sperm, the female usually chases him down and captures him and eats him to provide nutrients for the developing young."

"Like, wraps him up and dissolves him with acid like prey?"

"Yes," Teracht said solemnly.

Jesus, I suddenly realized why Teracht had been so eager to get away from the monster world. His whole life would have been catching prey, breaking off his dick inside of a female if he could even incapacitate her with his size, and then likely getting dissolved into a puddle of spider meat. "That sounds like a really shitty existence."

"I do not disagree," Teracht said with a chuckle, rolling over onto his stomach and retracting his bulbous dick inside of him.

"What happens if the male gets away?" I asked.

"I know a few have," he mused thoughtfully. "Since they have mated and cannot do so again, they basically will spend the rest of their lives as they did before, hunting prey, but they will also become targets for other spiders to attack them. Losing one's penis creates a change in our scent and tends to attract unwanted attention from spiders and other predators."

"Fuck," I said. "But you are so intelligent. Atauri don't have like cities, technology, ways to express themselves like art or music or anything?"

Teracht shook his head. "The monster world is a very unforgiving place for many."

"I'm sorry," I said.

"It's all right," Teracht said, giving me a sweet smile. "I am here now, and I do not intend to go back. I like it here. With you."

"I like you being here," I said, just as the doorbell rang. I checked my phone to see a notification that my delivery was on its way, so that was probably it. "That's my stuff, I'll be right back."

I went to the front door, unlocking it, finding the bags from the store on the stoop and the delivery car already headed away. I brought the bags inside. "I'm going to go brush my teeth and put on some deodorant," I said. "I'll be right back."

Teracht nodded and took the bags with the food as I went up to the bathroom. I stared thoughtfully into the mirror as I brushed my teeth. Teracht's life would have been so different in the monster world, but he was here now, in the human world, with all its pleasures and safety. And he still managed to be sweet, excited, and kind, despite the sort of life a spider creature seemed to have to endure in such an unforgiving land. I didn't know how he did it. But he also had finally put himself out there to meet someone, and I was not going to let him down. Everything else in my life was in shreds, but Teracht was new, and he was willing to adjust his life to share friendship with me, and maybe even more. It was nice to not be alone anymore. I had thought that, after my friends abandoned me, I would be alone forever, with no one to care for me or love me for who I was. But Teracht wasn't judging me. He was even adapting his life to accommodate me. We both could use a friend right now.

Chapter 10

Teracht

I HAD BEEN WORRIED after I showed Caleb what I had for genitals, thinking perhaps he might not be interested in being with me anymore, but he came down from the bathroom smelling of mint and something fresh under his armpits and grinned at me. "Okay, I was thinking about it. I agree, I don't think our anatomies are compatible if I could snap off your dick accidentally, and if it doesn't feel good to you anyway, it might just not be your thing."

I smiled weakly at him. "I wish it felt good so I could give you pleasure," I said wistfully.

"You *do* give me pleasure," Caleb protested. He moved over in front of my web and held up his arms. I scooped him up, carrying him further into the mass of webbing before settling him into it next to me. "What feels good to you?"

I blinked at the question. "What do you mean?"

"Is there anything you do, or some spot I touch you, that feels good? It doesn't have to be sexual or anything. But maybe there's a way you can feel good too."

I leaned in to rest my cheek on his shoulder. "I did enjoy tying you up," I said softly. "It made me feel something I haven't felt before. And when you struggle, it goes through my web, and it... it feels good. I feel powerful, like you are my prey. Not that I would ever hurt you!" I added hastily.

"I know you wouldn't, don't worry." He reached up to press his palm to my cheek. His skin was so warm and soft, and I leaned into his touch. "So, you do like tying me up."

"Yes. Did *you* like it?" I asked hesitantly.

Caleb nodded. "Yeah, I did. It was a little weird, I'll admit, but not bad. Your webs are also just really cool. I like how they feel. They actually make me feel good. All the pressure is off my injuries, and that is just... It's a relief."

I smiled. I didn't like Caleb in pain. "You are welcome to use my web any time you'd like," I offered.

"Thanks, Ter," he said, giving me a grin. "So, what do you want to do to me when I'm tied up and at your mercy?"

All of my eyes blinked, my hands coming up to press to my cheeks, as if to shove away the blush that suddenly heated them. "I..."

"Come on, tell me. I'm not a prude or anything," Caleb said.

I cleared my throat. "I would like to wrap you up in my

webbing so you can't move, and then..."

"And then?" he prompted.

I shook my head. "No. It's not proper of me."

"Fuck that," Caleb said, sitting up and tossing his hair. "It's just you and me here. Tell me what you want."

Heat was surging through me, so much I thought I might set myself aflame. "I want you to be under my control, and then I want to pleasure you, until you can't even remember your own name."

Caleb stared at me, and I felt my whole body crumple in on itself. "I'm sorry. That is so presumptuous of me."

"No, I- Huh." Caleb looked thoughtful, giving me a small smirk. "Little spider has big dom dreams."

I was going to drop dead from all the heat in my face. "I'm sorry."

"No! Ter." Caleb reached out his hand and placed it lightly on my forearm. "I told you to be honest. So, thank you for sharing that with me."

I cleared my throat. His hand on my arm was so warm and soft. "It's just a fantasy. I don't need anything like that from you."

"Hey, we talked about this. There's nothing wrong with fantasies, and this is one that could actually work. I mean, it's simple enough."

"But would you enjoy it?" I asked. The idea of being tied up myself was terrifying, but that was an ingrained response to what my life had been back in the monster world, where incapacitation meant death. Not here, and not with Caleb.

Caleb grinned. "Having a big, sexy monster tie me up and pleasure me? I mean, that sounds pretty hot."

No one had ever said I was 'sexy' before, and I was sure my entire body was blushing. "But I couldn't pleasure you with my penis."

"No, but there's plenty of other ways," Caleb said, reaching out and taking one of my hands. He studied my pointed fingertips for a moment, seeming to be thinking. "Just have to be a little careful, but I've got some ideas, if you're interested."

"Yes, I want to hear them!" I said, probably much too eagerly, and Caleb laughed, leaning in to kiss me. I kissed him back, running my fingers through his hair.

We spent the next half hour browsing online, Caleb adding a few things to his online shopping cart and then checking out with Same Day Delivery. What a world this was where one could get sex toys delivered in only a few hours. We then curled up on my web and watched television together. I couldn't fully concentrate on the show as I held Caleb close to me, playing my fingers through his hair. He was so beautiful and had been so sweet and kind to me in my naiveté. I wanted to make him feel good. Even though I did not feel a sexual thrill from stimulation the way humans did, it still thrilled me to see them in so much pleasure, and I wanted Caleb to feel pleasure like that. I was sure it would take time and practice, but he didn't seem like he was going anywhere.

Lunchtime came, and Caleb made himself some food with the groceries he had delivered. We stood in the kitchen as he nibbled on his food, and I drank several bottles of liquids. He had gotten a bottle of some new fruit juice I did not know, and he gladly poured some into a glass for me to try as well. I was learning so many new flavors from him, and it was delightful! It had taken me a little time to figure out what tasted good to me and what did not in the human world, and what ensured I got the nutrition I needed. But I was beginning to understand more of how food could be pleasurable instead of just for survival.

"What is your favorite food?" I asked him as we cleaned up the last remnants of the meal.

Caleb thought for a moment. "I like all kinds of stuff. But I think my favorite kind of food is Chinese."

"What is Chinese?" I asked.

"Fried rice, lots of meat and vegetables in different kinds of sauces," he said. "There's a place not too far from my apartment that has the best egg rolls ever."

"How does one roll an egg?" I asked curiously, and he pulled out his phone to show me. An egg roll looked nothing like an egg. "Are there eggs in it?" I asked him.

"You are making me have to Google so much more stuff than I ever used to," Caleb said with a dramatic sigh, typing into his phone. After a moment, he replied, "No, not anymore."

"Then why is it called an egg roll?" I asked in confusion.

"Because that's what it was called like a hundred years ago, and the name just stuck, I guess," Caleb said, scanning his phone.

I sighed. "That is very confusing. But it looks like it might be tasty."

"It is," Caleb replied. He looked at me thoughtfully. "You can only eat liquids and really, really soft stuff, right?"

I nodded. "I have tried some soft foods like yogurts and applesauce, and I can eat those pretty easily. But liquids are much easier for me to mix protein into."

"Yeah, I can understand that," Caleb replied. "Can I ask you a question?"

"Shoot," I said, and he chuckled, giving my shoulder a nudge.

"If you could go anywhere in the world, where would you go?"

I blinked. "I like Edgewind."

"Well, yeah. But if you could just travel the human world. Where would you want to go?"

I thought about all of the movies and things I had watched. I liked to watch documentaries about different countries and different eras in human history. The human world was so much bigger than this little town. But I had never been confident enough to even think about exploring it beyond the safe confines of our protected space. "I don't know," I finally said. "I think I would like to see everything.

Your world has so many different places and people. I think it would be fascinating to explore it all." I glanced over at him with a small smile. "Where would *you* want to go?"

"Hmm. I think I'm like you, I'd love to just travel the world. Though I'd love to see the old Egyptian pyramids, maybe go inside some of the old tombs. Pretend I was one of the not-stupid explorers in The Mummy."

"What is The Mummy?" I asked, and Caleb's eyes lit up.

"You never saw that?"

"No," I said.

"Fuck, I know what we're watching next," Caleb said.

I giggled softly. "Okay." I would watch anything Caleb wanted to, and seeing him excited about something made my insides dance.

We curled up in my web, and Caleb found the movie amongst my many streaming services. I nestled happily against him as we settled in to watch. "Oh, fuck, wait, there are bugs that eat people in this," he said, pausing it and turning to me with concern. "Is that okay?"

I rolled all eight of my eyes, even though I gave him a grateful smile. "Yes, Caleb, I am not upset by bugs eating people. Or movies with giant spiders, or movies where spiders are killed, or anything like that."

"Okay," Caleb said with relief. "Just wanted to be sure."

We sat and watched the movie, which was very exciting, and I was even more delighted by Caleb's left hand resting on one of my legs for the entire thing, occasionally giving it a gentle squeeze without seeming to realize it.

It was a good movie, and Caleb told me about all of the actors he had had crushes on when he was younger. It was funny seeing him so animated about something, and it warmed my heart. "So, some humans like both males and females?" I asked.

Caleb nodded. "Yeah. Like me, I like males and females. What about you?"

I blinked. "I like you."

He blushed, and I realized I had said the same thing to him before. "Right, but are you attracted to men or women, or both?"

"I have no idea," I said honestly. "But you are attractive."

He stared at me, going quiet for a moment, and I wondered if I had said something wrong. "Can I ask you something?"

"Yes, of course." His voice was so soft that it had me worried.

"When you first met me and saw my... my injuries, what did you think of them?"

"I don't know," I admitted.

"Did they scare you? Or disgust you?"

"No," I said, reaching up to brush my fingertip over his right cheek. "I understand that this is not how most humans typically look. But it is how you look, and I like it, because I like you."

"Yeah?" he said, tipping his head more into my touch.

"Yes. I know you are not happy about it," I said, watching his face carefully for any signs that I might be saying something I shouldn't. "I know that you feel you lost something very important when you were in your accident. But one thing I learned in the monster world is that scars mean you survived. You fought your way free, and maybe you paid a price for it. But you're alive because you survived whatever was trying to hurt you. That doesn't mean that it doesn't hurt or that you aren't scared. But you still have your life, which is something you can't ever get back once it's lost."

"God, Ter," Caleb said, his blue eyes shimmering with a hint of tears. "You say some very profound shit."

I blinked. "I do? I am just trying to be honest."

"Well, your honesty is better than a lot of humans," he said, leaning in to kiss me. I kissed him back, curling him into my arms. I shifted to roll onto my back so he was resting on top of me, holding him carefully so he did not slide or fall. It was a strange, new feeling to have someone so warm and alive curled close to my abdomen, but I liked it. I could easily become addicted to the feeling of someone touching me, sleeping against me. Caleb ran his hand down my chest. I held still and let him explore every curve and plane that he wanted, my hand resting lightly on his back to hold him in place. "I haven't left my house a lot since the accident. Only when I have to. Thank you, for forcing me to step outside my comfort zone."

"I don't want to force you to do anything," I said, brushing his cheek gently. "But I am happy you decided to come over and that you were not afraid of me."

"Same," he said, leaning in to kiss me. "So, um, are we dating now?"

I blinked. "Are you asking if you are my boyfriend?"

"Yeah, I guess I am," Caleb said.

That sent a good feeling that I couldn't easily describe through me. Being boyfriends was part of romance, and while my own experiences with romance were limited to what I saw on television, I knew it signaled a big step in our relationship. "I would like for you to be my boyfriend," I said, gazing back at him and feeling my heartbeat pick up a little in my chest. "But I've never had one before, and I'm not entirely sure what I'm supposed to do. Is that all right?"

"Yeah," Caleb said. "One awesome thing about humans is that we get to make decisions about our lives. So, we can decide what dating means to us and what makes us happy, and we don't have to follow anyone else's rules."

It was another experiment, like trying the chocolate milkshake, or joining the monster dating app. But it was an experiment we were going to do together. I would do or try anything if Caleb kept spending time with me. "You make me happy," I said. I held out my left hand to him. "Boyfriends?"

Caleb took it in his own, giving it a firm shake. "Boyfriends," he agreed, and his smile was like sunshine warming my skin.

Chapter 11

Caleb

We cuddled for a while, until we heard the tell-tale thump of a package being set down on the doorstep. We opened the box, and I pulled each thing out, Teracht cutting the packages open with one of his spidery legs. We hadn't gone too crazy just yet. A dildo, a vibrating butt plug with a remote, some lube, some cotton balls, and a box of black nitrile gloves. Pretty basic stuff, but easy to work with while we explored this new aspect of our relationship. It had been a while since I had bottomed, and I was feeling a little nervous, especially since I was the only one between us with that sort of experience. But Teracht seemed eager to learn. I went upstairs to take another shower with my new soap and shampoo, glad I had added a set of towels to my delivery so I could dry off easily this time.

Once I was clean all over, I headed back downstairs, not bothering to get dressed. I didn't make a habit of wandering around naked in my apartment, so I did feel a bit self-conscious, but Teracht's appreciative glance over my body as I came down the stairs and into the living room made any discomfort vanish. Teracht had washed and set aside all of the toys, but he had waited for me to take the nitrile gloves out. I pushed a cotton ball into the tip of each of the fingers before helping him to slide the glove onto his hand. "All right?" I asked.

"It feels weird," Teracht admitted, flexing his hand experimentally before brushing his fingertips over his other palm. "But I don't think I'll hurt you this way."

I nodded. "I trust you. We'll take it slow, and I promise I'll tell you if anything hurts."

"And I want you to tell me if something feels good, so I know I am pleasuring you the right way," Teracht said, sounding a little shy.

"I will," I reassured him.

Teracht leaned in to kiss me. "And we'll stop if you want to."

"Right," I said, standing on my toes to kiss him sweetly in return. Once I drew back, he slid his arms around me and lifted me off my feet, climbing onto his web and carrying me like I was nothing but a rag doll under his arm. I was still very disconcerted that he could do that, but, at the same time, it also made me strangely horny, to know I could be overpowered so easily by him but that he chose not to.

Teracht settled me into the center of one of his webs, then produced one of the couch pillows he must have grabbed with one of his spider feet. "Find a comfortable position, pet. You're going to be in it for a long time."

A shiver of pleasure ran through me at those words. "Yes, sir," I said. Teracht waited while I shifted, trying to find a position that was comfortable on my wounds but still kept both my ass and my dick accessible to him. I finally settled the pillow under my stomach and stretched out over it, spreading my legs wide and supporting myself Sphynx-like with my arms. I gave Teracht a nod once I was in a comfortable spot. Quick as a flash, he was suddenly on top of me, looping strands of webbing around my wrists and forearms to keep them from moving, several thick lashes around my chest and stomach so I couldn't pull or arch up, and then around my ankles, keeping my legs spread wide and slightly bent for him. He was so damn fast, it was almost scary. But when he was done, he leaned down to plant a kiss on my right shoulder.

"Everything all right, pet?"

"Yeah," I said, then quickly added, "sir."

I felt more than saw Teracht smile at that. "And you're going to tell me how you're feeling, aren't you, pet?"

"Yes, sir," I said. My stomach was doing flip-flops. I hadn't been this nervous in bed in years. Not that I didn't trust Teracht; I was sure he would listen to me if something wasn't all right. But this whole thing suddenly felt much more loaded with the understanding we were in a relationship now and that he wanted to ensure he was bringing me pleasure. That felt like a lot of pressure, even if most of my job was to lie there and take it. That thought made my muscles tighten just a little as heat ran down my spine.

He rubbed the smooth plane of his cheek against one of the round globes of my ass. "When was the last time you did this, pet?"

"Mm. It's been a while, sir," I said. "Probably almost a year."

And then I jumped, though couldn't move too far, when Teracht gave a light nip to the skin of my other ass cheek with his flat palate.

"Good or bad?" Teracht prompted.

"Good," I said softly.

I figured he might, with his little experience, immediately try to stick his fingers in me, and I prepared myself for that. But he surprised me again when he placed both of his hands on my ass cheeks, spreading them wide, before he pressed a kiss to the small of my back. I squirmed, feeling the web vibrate under me, and he must have felt it too, because he moaned quietly and kissed me again there before the tip of his tongue drifted out to brush over my hole. I made a very undignified squeaking noise, and Teracht's movements paused. "Good?"

"Mm, so good," I said, pressing my cheek onto the web

under me.

"Keep going?" he purred.

"Please," I said, and his tongue began to wander in my crease, over each bit of sensitive skin. He found my hole again with the tip of it and circled it. I tensed and let out a soft moan as kneaded my ass with his hands. He suddenly ran one of his spider feet over the sole of my foot to tickle me. I groaned, body tensing, toes curling as I instinctively struggled to pull away from the tickling, but his webbing held me secure, and I was entirely at Teracht's mercy.

He continued to lick and poke my hole with his tongue, not entering me, just making me squirm and writhe beneath him in my trapped position, legs occasionally jerking as he brushed the soles of my feet. And then his left hand wrapped around my cock and gave it a tentative squeeze. I gasped, my body suddenly torn between wanting to push back into his mouth and forward into his hand. "All right?" he asked.

"Yes, sir," I groaned, and he rewarded me with another prod of his tongue to my hole. He tickled my foot again, and I tensed, just as he gave my cock a stroke. I let out a sharp gasp.

He pulled back just a bit to ask, "Good or bad?"

"Good," I groaned, even as my foot quivered, trying to pull away from his teasing.

"You're supposed to be telling me what feels good, pet," Teracht reminded me before running his tongue up the length of my crack.

"Y... Yes, sir, I'm sorry," I gasped.

He suddenly pulled back from me, and I couldn't stop a disappointed sound, trying to turn my head to see what he was doing.

"Eyes forward, pet," he told me, and I flushed and turned my head away. I heard the snap of the lube bottle opening, and my body gave a quiver of nervous anticipation.

His left hand, with the cold lube, closed around my cock again, making me jump. "Fuck," I groaned, my hips trying to press into his touch. And then two of his gloved fingers, covered in lube, slid down the crease of my ass, making me tense. "Yes, please."

His hand slid away from my cock, the air much too cool without him, and I whimpered. He kissed the small of my back. "Don't worry, pet, I'll not leave you wanting. I just don't want you moving around too much when I'm trying to use my fingers."

"Th... that's fair," I groaned, and he didn't seem to mind my less formal reply. I knew I was going to be tight, even bent at the angle I was, and he was doing this for the first time too.

He pressed one finger firmly to my entrance, but it did not push inside. I groaned softly, trying not to move, baring down as much as I could. "Getting inside is going to take more pressure. You're not hurting me."

"All right," he said, his left hand, cool and sticky with lube stroking over my left hip. His finger pressed harder, and he finally slid inside of me. I exhaled as the movement became easier, his finger pressing deeper. I felt myself tremble, and the web gave a responding vibration.

"Yes," I moaned, and he pressed a kiss to one of my ass cheeks. "That's good."

He chuckled softly and drew his finger back before slowly pushing in again. "Like that?"

"Yeah," I said. He started up a slow rhythm of moving his finger inside of me. I did my best to relax for him, the initial burn subsiding as his finger slid in and out of me and coated my passage with lube. He gave his finger a little experimental curl inside of me, and I gasped, my fingers clenching into a fist. "Yes," I moaned.

"You like that," he commented, and I nodded eagerly. "But human penises, and the toy we bought, don't do that."

"No," I agreed. "But it doesn't all have to be... nngh... be the same in order to feel good."

"Ah, I see," he said, giving his finger an experimental twist that had me gasping, my legs trying to squirm against the webbing that held me, but I was going nowhere.

Suddenly a second finger pressed inside of me. I winced and let out a sharp gasp, and Teracht instantly pulled his entire hand away. "I'm sorry, did I hurt you?"

"No," I said, my hips pushing back, trying to find his hand again. "That was just a little fast. I promised I'd tell you if you hurt me."

"Oh. I'm sorry."

"Teracht, stop apologizing, it's just fine," I said, dropping any pretense that might have been there. I turned my head as best I could, only able to see him out of the corner of my eye but knowing he could see all of me with his extended vision. "It felt good. Start with one again, and then add a second one with more lube."

Teracht nodded and dutifully added another healthy squirt of lube to his fingers. I wondered if lube came off webbing or if he was going to have to remake whole sections of the room after we were done. I turned my head forward, pressing myself down into the pillow under me and letting the bonds of the web hold me in place. Teracht's finger slid in easily this time, working inside of me before he cautiously added a second finger. It burned a little from the stretch, and I groaned softly. "Yeah, good, just like that," I said as his fingers slid back and forth inside of me. He pressed a kiss to my lower back, and then nipped my left ass cheek as his fingers glided in and out, my passage sticky with lube. I made a rather ungraceful sound when he nibbled me, and he laughed, which made me relax further.

Then his other hand wrapped around my shaft, and he was stroking my dick in time with the thrust of his fingers so that when he pushed his fingers in, the movement pushed my hips down into his other hand. "Yeah," I groaned, my fingers clenching, my eyes closing. "Fuck, yeah."

Teracht hummed a little sound of approval, and the movements of his hands became faster. My legs quivered under his ministrations, my abs clenching too as I rested on the pillow. I pressed my face onto the webbing below me, my forehead already sticky with sweat. "Yes," I groaned. For only learning about human sexuality a short time ago, my little spider was a quick study and seemed to be reading my movements. Pleasure was already building in my lower belly, and I knew I wasn't going to last long at this rate. "Please, sir, can I come?" I moaned.

Teracht's movements suddenly slowed. "No, pet, you can't. We've barely gotten started."

He had a point, and it wasn't like I wanted this to end so soon. Teracht seemed to be enjoying himself too, at least. His fingers inside of me curled just a bit, and I mewled in pleasure. He laughed softly. "Can you take a third finger, pet, or is that too much?"

"I can take it. Sir," I added hastily.

Teracht moved his left hand off my cock to rest it on my hip, and then I felt the press of a third finger into my tight hole. I tensed a moment. God, it had been way too long since I had that much inside of me, but damn, did it feel good once my body relaxed around them. And when he began to move his fingers, but not all together like he had been, my hips arched back into him. "Fuck, yes, whatever you're doing, don't stop," I whined, and he laughed, his finger movements continuing as his left hand stroked over my back, up and down my spine. I felt his sharp fingertips brush lightly over my skin, sending a tingle through every spot they touched. They continued to travel over my back and hips and the soft parts of my left side, caressing each inch of skin as they brushed it, as gentle as the first time he explored me. My arms strained against the webs that held them as he moved, and I heard Teracht moan as the vibrations went through them. That sent even more pleasure through me, knowing that he was feeling good too. I shoved my ass backward as far as I could with my restraints. "More," I begged.

His hands suddenly stilled on me, and I cried out in frustration. "I will give you all you want, pet, but in my own time." God, his voice was killing me with his teasing. My shy little spider was definitely coming into his own here.

"Please," I moaned. "Please, sir."

"Mm. My pet is asking so nicely. But we haven't even gotten to play with your toys yet."

Fuck, I had forgotten about those. I moaned, arching my back again. Teracht gave the back of my right thigh a soft lick, making me jump. "Do you want to try some of those, pet?"

"If you'd like to, sir," I forced out, my breath a little shaky.

"Would that give you pleasure?" Teracht asked, giving my cock another gentle stroke.

"Yes, sir," I gasped.

And then his hands were gone from me, everywhere, a bit of a burn in my ass from his fingers leaving me so quickly. I squirmed, hearing the snap of the lube bottle opening and the slick sound of it coating what I assumed was the dildo. I was proven right when Teracht was back behind me and pressing it against my still stretched hole. It wasn't a small one, but it wasn't any bigger than his fingers had been, and it sank in easily, making me gasp and writhe. Teracht pushed it all the way in until the base of it was pressed flush against my ass cheeks. "Fuck," I groaned, drawing the word out as the cool silicone filled my passage. It started to slide out, and Teracht seemed to realize he had to hold it in place as his hand stroked over my cock lovingly. "Do you like this, pet?"

"Yes, sir," I moaned, my hips pushing back as best I could in my trapped position.

Teracht let the dildo slide almost out before pushing it back in, starting up a maddeningly slow rhythm that made my toes curl as each inch moved in and out of me. "God, yes," I groaned. "Faster, please."

Teracht moved it a little faster inside of me, pushing it deeper with each thrust, making me moan and writhe under him, my stomach digging into the pillow. Not being able to move with my whole body constrained by his webs was maddening as I desperately wanted to push my hips back into each thrust to take it deeper and faster. Teracht giggled softly. "Does it pleasure you more when it is faster?"

How did he expect me to answer that coherently in my current state? "Yes, sir," I gasped, then couldn't stop a frustrated whine when he slowed the thrusting down again. His hand stroked over my cock as he moved the dildo inside of me, pausing to grind it against me. I inhaled sharply, my eyes closing. "Fuck, yes."

"Mm, I like the pretty noises you make, pet," Teracht

said, leaning down to suddenly run his tongue up my right shoulder. It was a strange sensation, feeling different than it did on my uninjured skin, but not an unpleasant feeling. "How does that feel?" he asked, the tip of his tongue sneaking out to brush my earlobe.

"Weird. Do it again?" I asked, and Teracht obliged, taking a long, slow lick up my shoulder.

"Different," I said. "But not bad."

Teracht gave the side of my neck a gentle kiss. "And this?"

My eyes closed as tears suddenly threatened to spill for no reason. "Good."

Teracht's tongue brushed over the pulse point in my neck, then gave me an ever-so-gentle nip with his flat palate before soothing it with his tongue. I realized as heat surged inside of me that the movement of his hands had stilled, and he was focused on just that spot, nuzzling his face into it. One of his spider feet suddenly moved to stroke over my right side, over my ribs and down my side to my hip, then back up. He kissed and nibbled gently at my throat and jaw, every movement careful and deliberate as he gauged my reaction.

I opened my eyes, turning them to watch his leg brushing up and down my side. It was a strange sight, and yet, it made my blood heat in my veins. "You are so beautiful, pet," Teracht whispered, giving my earlobe a gentle nip followed by a loving caress with his tongue. "Absolutely stunning, and I am so lucky to have you." His hand began to stroke over my cock again, slow and sensual, starting up another lazy rhythm with thrusting the toy inside of me so I felt every inch enter and retreat from me. "And I am going to tell you that every day until you believe me."

I pressed my forehead against the webs under me, tears prickling my lashes, but I would not let them fall. I had done enough crying at Teracht's house, even if the tears were partially from happiness. He ran his tongue up my side, tickling my ribs and making me squirm, and he let out a soft moan as the web rippled beneath us. "Yes, my pet," he cooed, his hands starting to move faster on me. "Let me show you how beautiful you are."

God, his words fucking broke me inside as heat built under my skin. He wasn't afraid of me, and he didn't find my body scary or disgusting or something to be hidden away. He touched every inch of it as if it were precious. He didn't want to hurt me, but he didn't handle me like I was a pane of glass that could shatter at any moment either. "Please," I said softly, my fingers curling. "Please touch me."

And then his hands were all over, still pumping my cock and the toy inside of me, but his spider legs were wrapped around me, several pairs holding himself snugly against me as other ones roamed over my skin, touching, teasing, flicking, dragging, until every touch felt like I was being licked by the most delicious flames. His spider feet flicked over my nipples, drew patterns on my skin, ran through my hair. I cried out, writhing under him, feeling him press down harder on top of me as the dildo fucked even harder into me, drawing a wail of pleasure from my lips. "Teracht, please! Please, I need to come," I begged, and he gave the back of my neck a soft nip.

"Come for me, pet," he whispered in my ear, stroking me so hard and fast that when I came only seconds later, my entire vision went white for several moments. I ever so slowly became aware of Teracht nestling on top of me, one of his legs stroking my hair, but everything else, all of his other touches on me, were still. My ass still spasmed around the toy inside me, but he only held it still now, letting me ride out the waves of pleasure as little jolts raced through me. I forgot how to breathe for a moment as my heart thundered, several drops of sweat creeping down my forehead and cheek.

I finally came back to myself. The webbing under me was so light that I could hardly use it to focus as I dragged my soul back into my body, taking a deep breath like I had been drowning. Teracht's weight on top of me was warm and comforting but caused no pain in my body, just the feel of us touching so intimately.

After a few minutes of neither of us doing anything besides breathing, Teracht gave my neck a gentle kiss. "Doing all right?"

"Y... Yeah," I said, trying to form words. Hell, even coherent syllables. "'Sgood..."

Teracht laughed and shifted on top of me, his weight and heat suddenly gone but not causing the web to shift at all beneath me. He started to draw the dildo out of me, but the sensation made me cry out and tense around it, and he stopped, running his pointed fingertips down my back. "Not yet?"

"Not yet," I agreed, laying still for his touch, which was the only thing I wanted right now. "Holy... fuck... God..."

Teracht giggled and traced my spine lightly. "Just breathe, pet. You don't have to move until you're ready."

I debated never moving again, just lying here on this web forever. That sounded pretty damn good right now. But eventually I started to feel extremely sticky, the lube and my come drying on my skin, and I had to imagine that Teracht was probably feeling the same way. "Okay, take it out, just slow," I said. Teracht obediently slid the toy out of me, leaving me feeling boneless beneath him. One of his feet moved by me and slit the webbing that held me bound in place.

"Can you get up?" he asked.

"Maybe?" I said, giving my legs an experimental stretch. Teracht slid his arm under me and pulled me up to my knees. I hissed softly as tenderness went through my ass. Fuck, I was going to feel that the rest of the weekend. And that was totally fine by me. I leaned back into his embrace, and several of his legs went around me.

"Are you doing all right?" he asked. I tipped my head back to look up at him, finding all eight of his onyx eyes staring concernedly down at me.

"Yeah," I said, shifting a little to get feeling back into all of my muscles. "Yeah, I'm great. That was amazing."

Teracht beamed, then carefully scooped me up in his arms to carry me across his web and down to the ground. He started to set me on the couch. "No, I'm sticky!" I protested, but he only laid me on my back on the couch anyway, the other pillow under my head.

"Rest. I'll go clean up, and then you can shower."

He produced a blanket from next to the couch, draping it over me, and I didn't protest, just nestled under the warmth and closed my eyes. He brushed a kiss over my forehead, and then he moved away and headed upstairs.

Chapter 12

Teracht

After cleaning up and eating some food, Caleb was more than content to curl up on my web and watch TV until he fell asleep. I smiled to myself as I pulled a blanket over him, using a few quick threads to secure it so it didn't slide off of him, before going about my usual nightly business, tearing down any old or damaged webs and replacing them. I napped a bit as the night drew on, but whenever I woke, the first thing I did was check on Caleb. He slept contentedly, a tiny snore occasionally coming from him when he fell into a deeper sleep. He was so trusting of me, curled up asleep in my web, allowing me to tie him up and do things to him, especially with my lack of experience and knowledge of human sexuality. I would never ever want to hurt him. I only wanted him to feel good, to feel pleasure at my hands.

When he woke up in the morning, he showered and put on clean clothes before coming to the kitchen to join me for breakfast. We still had at least all of today to spend together, and while I wasn't sure what we would do yet, I would be happy to do anything at all with him by my side.

"Do you have like a backyard?" Caleb asked curiously, glancing toward the back door as he finished his food and I finished my beverages.

I nodded slowly. "It is small, it just leads to the alley where the trash pickup is. But there's a little area out there."

"Do you ever sit outside?" Caleb asked.

I blinked, then shook my head. "No."

"Why not?" Caleb seemed surprised.

I shrugged. "I like being inside better."

Caleb gazed at me for a moment before he held out his hand. "Would you sit outside with me?"

I blinked my humanoid eyes. "There's nothing out there for you to sit on."

"Then I guess it's good I have a big, strong spider to make something for me," he said, his voice sweet and coaxing, and I laughed. I supposed I could easily make him a seat out there.

"All right."

We headed outside, stepping into the sunshine. The air was crisp but not cold, the weather starting to warm up. I had a small patch of grass as the backyard, with a pavestone path leading to the alley, the entire property surrounded by a white picket fence, which pleased me to no end. There was a sort of wooden awning over the back door, and a concrete patio slab that was really only big enough for a couple chairs and a table, if I ever put something out there. I never spent time on the patio. My 'going outside' consisted of taking my trash and recycling out and then retreating back inside.

Caleb inhaled and stretched his arms over his head. "Mm. I love spring."

I wrapped my arms around his waist to pull him back against me, pressing a kiss to his shoulder. I suddenly realized that Caleb was outside with only a tank top on top, exposing his scarred arm and shoulder, as well as his neck and face, to anyone who could see us. Granted, we were on my property, but he was feeling comfortable enough to let his insecurities go for the moment, and I could too. My heart gave a little flutter.

"Should I make a seat for you?" I asked, and he nodded, leaning against one of the wooden posts to watch me. I knew I could just do a simple hammock, but I was feeling like showing off a little. So, I climbed up until I was clinging to the ceiling of the overhang. I moved over to Caleb, shifting to lean so I could kiss him upside down. He grinned and reached up to hold my cheek with his hand as he kissed me back.

"I am not going to make a Spider-Man joke," he said with a straight face when we pulled apart. I narrowed my eyes at him, and he just gave me a smirk. "So, how do you stick to the ceiling when there's no webbing there?"

"I don't know," I said, lifting up one of my feet to examine it, as if I had never seen them before. Not that I often spent that much time focused on my own feet. "It is natural for me, so I suppose there is something on my feet that allows me to stay there." I began to spin, drawing webbing from my spinnerets and securing it to the wood.

Caleb watched me in fascination, and I couldn't help flaunting a little, tossing the loops more for him to see, weaving a more decorative pattern than I normally would. Once the main line was long enough and secure, I climbed down it and began to weave the frame of the chair for him. I remembered seeing those funny-looking egg-like chairs on TV and in online stores. I could easily make something like that, and it seemed like something Caleb would appreciate. "Do you feel different being upside down?" Caleb asked as he watched me.

"No," I said. "Does it feel different for humans?"

"Oh yeah," he said, brushing his fingers through his hair that was still a little damp from his shower. "All the blood rushes to your head, and it can cause a lot of pressure. Some people even pass out if they are upside down."

"Do you?" I asked curiously as I shaped the outer frame.

"Do I what?"

"Pass out."

"I haven't," Caleb said thoughtfully. "But I'd much rather be right side up."

I giggled softly. Caleb upside down might be pretty cute,

with his hair falling. It would probably look like mine then. I would have to try that later, as long as I didn't hurt him.

"What are you laughing at?" Caleb asked, raising a brow.

"Just imagining you upside down."

"Hmm. I used to be able to do a handstand," he said. "I never tried it one-handed though. I don't know if I have enough strength in my one arm to support me anymore. And I'd rather not break my one good wrist to try."

"I would prefer that as well," I said. "Although, then I'd have to bundle you up and take care of you. Feed you, bathe you. You would be my little pet for sure."

Caleb snorted softly. "You're all about this 'pet' thing."

I paused in my weaving for a moment to look over at him with more than just one eye. "I have never had a pet. Any sort of domestic animal would be considered prey to me in the monster world."

"Would you want a pet?" Caleb asked curiously. "Like, a dog or a cat or something? A tarantula?" He gave me another smirk.

I flicked my foot at him, sending a piece of webbing right into his face, and he yelped, arms flailing as he tried to get it off of him. I laughed as he huffed and straightened his hair. "Maybe one day. When I know that I would not react instinctively and hurt it."

"You don't do that with me," Caleb said.

"I know, but you're different. More intelligent."

"Aw, you say the sweetest things," Caleb teased.

I leaned over to give him a quick peck on the cheek before returning to my weaving. The frame was done, I was just adding in the crosshatches so he could lean back in it. "I do miss the chase part of hunting, but I'd be afraid of hurting an animal that was as small as a dog or cat." Humans were a bit sturdier in their construction, even if they weren't as flexible.

"What do you mean, the chase? I thought you caught stuff in your web to eat," Caleb said.

"I did. But sometimes something would manage to get free or would get caught in a part of my web that wasn't sticky enough to hold it. And sometimes-" I blushed a little, dropping all of my eyes away from him. "I would just get bored, and it was something to do."

"I have to imagine that was pretty terrifying for whatever you were stalking," Caleb said, and I nodded, heat filling my cheeks.

"I am sure it was. I am ashamed of it now."

"You didn't know any better, Ter," Caleb said. "I've never been to the monster world, but I'm sure the rules are very different than they are here."

"Yes," I agreed. "I much prefer to not have to kill things for survival."

"You have a good heart," Caleb replied. "What you do here is more important than what you did in the past to survive." I beamed at him, shifting to weave a quick, tight interior piece that he could sit on. "You really are amazing," he added, and the praise made my whole body shiver the tiniest bit.

"Thank you," I said with a slight blush. I gave the chair a quick yank to make sure it was solid, then motioned for Caleb to climb into it. He did, settling back inside of it. When I let go, it began to swing ever so gently. He sighed and tucked his legs up under him.

"This is great, thank you, Ter."

I nodded, settling onto my stomach next to him. "I'm glad you like it."

"I love it," Caleb replied, running his finger over one of the strands and giving it a twang, as if to test its stability. "Your webs are incredible too. Whatever they get used for, I bet they will be really helpful for humanity."

"I hope so," I said. "I want to help people if I can."

Caleb nodded thoughtfully, uncurling one leg to give the seat another push to make it swing a little more. "I don't know what I'm going to do now."

"Now that you're not modeling?" I asked.

"Yeah. I never finished college, or even really decided on a major. I loved modeling. And there was always the possibility of moving on to acting or something like that."

"Would you go back to it if you could?" I asked.

He nodded. "Yeah. I liked my old life. Although," he lifted his head to gaze at me, "If I hadn't been in my accident, I probably wouldn't have met you."

I frowned. "I want you to be happy."

"I *am* happy," he said, stopping his swinging and leaning over to grab my arm lightly in his hand. "I can't change what happened to me, so there's no reason for me to fixate on it. I've met you, and I'm glad I did. I'm just too much in my own head."

I blinked, then gave him a smile that I hoped looked sexy and wicked. "Would you like me to get you out of your head?"

"You have an idea?" he asked, and I nodded. "Okay," he said, getting to his feet.

"Come on," I said, giving him a pull inside the house. "Get naked."

"Again?" Caleb chuckled. "You went from a porn virgin to a sex fiend overnight."

I stared at him with concern. Was I pushing him too much too quickly? "Is that all right?"

Caleb laughed and moved into the living room. "Yes, Ter, it's just fine. It's just funny to me. But I like how oddly obsessed you get with stuff." He stood on his toes to give me a quick peck on the mouth before he shed his clothes and dumped them onto the couch. Reassured, I moved over to the small pile of toys we had collected. I picked up the vibrating plug and the bottle of lube. "Bend over the couch arm and spread your legs for me, pet."

Caleb shivered. "Yes, sir," he said, moving to follow my instructions. He spread his legs, giving me perfect access to his gorgeous ass. I leaned in and gave his asshole a lick with my tongue, which made him moan and writhe a little, before I spread the lube over the toy.

"Relax," I purred in his ear, running one of my legs down his side. He squirmed a bit, then gasped as I slid the stainless steel plug between his cheeks and pushed. He groaned and shifted a little, and I waited for him to adjust himself until he was in a better position. When he was, the toy sank inside of him, stretching him wide, and I watched it disappear into his ass with delight. Once the flared base rested against his ass cheeks, I gave one of them a light swat with my palm, and he let out a yelp, his hips grinding on the couch arm. I smiled to myself. Now to try something different and see if he would like it. I pulled some of my webbing into my hands and quickly wove it into a long, scarf-like piece. I brought it over his head, and then over his eyes. Caleb gasped, jerking a little. "All right?" I asked.

"Yeah." His voice trembled a bit, but he didn't sound afraid.

I lashed the webbing securely together at the back of his head, careful not to catch his hair, before I pulled back. "Now, come with me, pet."

Caleb straightened up from the couch with a soft moan, his hand going back to adjust the toy in his ass a little before he turned toward my voice. I took his arm and led him to my web, lifting him up with my legs. He gasped and clutched at me tightly, which sent a little thrill through my chest. I gave his neck a light nibble as we climbed up into my web.

"I won't let you fall." He nodded and held tighter to me as I crawled up higher. I found a nice spot and laid him down on the web. "Get comfortable."

He shifted around on his back, biting his lip as the plug must have moved inside of him. I stroked his hair until he had settled into a spot. And then I went to work, wrapping him up tightly in place, starting at his feet, and moving up his body. Caleb gasped, his hand reaching out toward me, but I pushed it gently back with one of my feet. "Hands down, pet. You can use your safe word if you want to, but otherwise, you need to trust me."

"Yes, sir." Caleb lowered his hand again, and I went back to cocooning him in the softest webbing I could make. I moved up his knees, pausing at his groin to give his cock a brush with my hand, which made him writhe a little and sent delicious pulses through my web, before I wrapped my webbing over his cock and his hips, enclosing them fully under the gossamer strands. Caleb whimpered softly, but it sounded more like disappointment than anything.

"It's all right, pet," I soothed as I continued to bind him, pinning his arms to his sides and working up his chest. "I promise you won't be wanting for long."

He inhaled softly. "What are you going to do, sir?"

"No, no," I said, brushing my finger over his lip. "You don't get to question me."

He flushed and went quiet, letting me work until I had wrapped him up to his neck. He looked like the mummies we had seen in his movie yesterday except for his head being free. I didn't want to wrap his head up, just left the blindfold in place. "Now, pet, you are going to relax," I said, giving his lips a soft brush with my own.

Caleb swallowed a bit. "I'll try, sir."

"Of course you will." And then I lifted the wireless remote that paired with the plug inside of him and hit the power button.

Caleb jerked like he had been slapped, the pulse of his body going through my web and making me hot all over. He gasped, and I could hear a faint buzzing from underneath the layers of webbing. His cheeks were pink, and he squirmed a little. "All right, pet?" I asked, stroking a hand over his hair.

Now that it was turned on, Caleb exhaled a breath and nodded slowly. "Yes, sir."

"Good. I'll be right here with you the whole time. But you are just going to lie there and relax and focus on nothing at all."

Caleb smiled a bit. "Yes, sir, I'll try."

"Good boy," I said, stroking his cheek gently before settling myself a few steps away. I could feel the tension in his body as I curled up onto my web, and I felt it slowly ebb away, bit by bit, as he laid there. I could feel each time he tensed just a bit, and I knew he was probably trying to not think. Smiling to myself, I hit the button on the remote. The pitch changed as it started to vibrate faster, and Caleb let out a moan, his body stiffening.

"Fuck. Ter, you're evil."

"I know," I said with a pleased smile that he couldn't see but could probably hear in my voice.

He squirmed a little, unable to move much with my web holding him in place, but I felt every little pulse and thrum, along with the constant vibration from the plug inside of him, all blending together to make the most beautiful symphony of vibrations. It was so delicious, I thought I might start drooling. He finally started to relax more fully, and I let him lie there for a few minutes, no movement except for the toy, before I hit the button again, and he jerked, letting out a yowl. "God! Ter!"

"Hmm?" I asked, as if I were not even paying attention to him.

Caleb shuddered. "How long are you going to torture me?"

"Am I torturing you?" I asked, feigning innocence.

"Yes," he whined, and I hit the button again. He let out a shout and jerked, but he wasn't going anywhere.

"As long as I please, pet. Don't worry. I'll let you come eventually."

"Goddammit," Caleb groaned through clenched teeth.

"Relax," I purred, plucking one of the webs to send the vibration through him, and Caleb whimpered, his breath coming in deep, quick pants. I hit the button again to bring the pulse down, and he moaned, trying to squirm but eventually settling into resolved stillness. Every once in a while, the sensation must have gotten to him, because he would give a little jerk or twitch, his ass muscles tensing. I let him lie there without doing anything for a very long time before I hit the button again to change the vibrations from constant to a sort of short pulse pattern. Caleb gasped and writhed. I wasn't sure how many patterns this toy had, but I was going to play with all of them and see what sorts of noises I could elicit from my trapped human.

Some of them I let go for minutes on end with no change, others only a few seconds before switching it. Each new sound or curse or movement I got out of Caleb delighted me. I wanted my human to stay out of his head for a while and just focus on the pleasure I could bring him. He deserved that happiness, and everything I could give him.

Caleb writhing and jerking on my web was sending waves of desire through me too. My mouth was watering, and I had to remind myself that this was pleasure, not prey. But as I watched him struggle against the bonds that held him, his muscles spasming in pleasure as he whined and moaned and cursed, I felt something inside me that I hadn't for a long time. The visceral desire to chase. To hunt. Not to kill; I hated that part. But the thrill of launching myself at prey, capturing it, wrapping it up, leaving it at my mercy, like Caleb was now. I missed that. I liked being lazy and having as much food as I could ever want at any time, but I was still a spider at heart, and that would never change.

Caleb had settled into almost stillness again, so I hit the

button to change the vibrations, and he let out a screech, jerking. "Ter! Fuck, please, please, can I come?"

I laughed softly. "You can take more pleasure, pet. A few more minutes, and then you can come."

Caleb let out a frustrated wail, and I moved over to him, giving him a kiss on the lips. "You're so mean," he whined, his body pulsing a bit as I changed the vibrations yet again. Tears of frustration were leaking from under his blindfold, and I kissed them away.

"And you like it, don't you, pet?" I cooed. When Caleb didn't answer, I ran my hand down over the bulge in the webbing where his erection was, making him jerk. "Don't you?"

"Yes, sir," he moaned, his hips trying to push up into my hand, but I pulled back, and he sank back down with a pleading whimper. "Please..."

"Mm. Tell me something you like about yourself, and then you can come."

"What?" Caleb asked in surprise.

"Tell me something you like about yourself," I repeated, emphasizing each word for him.

Caleb bit his lip, suddenly quiet. I hit the remote button, and he yelled, jerking against the webs that held him. "Fuck, I need to come, please, Ter!"

"I told you what you need to do so you can come," I said, brushing my thumb over his lower lip.

He let out a frustrated growl, and I just hit the button

again and backed away as he shuddered and mewled. His breath was coming in deep, erratic gasps, each jerk of his body a desperate plea, but I was not going to let him win this one. He either had to safe word out or do what I said. "Come on now, pet. Do you want to come or not?"

"Yes," he cried. "Please."

"Then, tell me," I said, letting one spider foot drift over his groin, feeling his cock pulsing and straining, and it made me dizzy with my own pleasure, the heat and scent of his arousal coursing through me.

Caleb made a small noise of ascent, and I left the toy setting where it was so as not to distract him. He squirmed hungrily against my web before he forced out, "I like that... that I am too stubborn to give up."

I beamed at the words. "I like that about you too," I said. I moved over to him, and, with a few quick movements of a foot, I had cut away the webbing that covered his groin. His cock sprang free, leaking clear fluid everywhere, and I couldn't resist the urge to close my mouth over the tip of it and suck.

The shout that came out of Caleb was divine as his hips jerked up into my mouth, and then he spilled his pleasure inside my mouth, over my tongue. I hadn't realized how much it would be, and some of it dripped down my chin as I swallowed what I could. I preferred sweeter flavors, but I could easily get used to the flavor of Caleb on my tongue every day. Beneath me, he let out a strangled sob of pleasure as his dick continued to pulse, the scent of sweat and passion mingling in the air around him. I leaned down and gave him a sticky kiss, and he eagerly swept his tongue into my mouth, panting against my lips as his tongue tangled with mine, tasting his own release. We kissed for a long time, until Caleb went almost limp under me except for the buzz of the plug still inside of him. When I finally pulled back from his lips, I turned it off, and Caleb nearly melted into my web, boneless and sweaty and spent. He looked absolutely gorgeous, his blond hair tousled, his cheeks streaked with lines from his tears of frustration and pleasure. I wanted him to always look that way, so satisfied and thoroughly fucked by my hand.

Caleb's breathing finally evened out, the little twitches of pleasure slowly turning into relaxed stillness. "All right, pet?" I asked gently, stroking a hand over his sweaty brow where a few strands of hair clung to the blindfold that still covered his eyes.

"Yes, sir," Caleb said, sounding drowsy.

"Do you want me to release you now?"

"Mm. Is it okay if I just stay here for a bit?" Caleb asked, and I smiled.

"Of course, pet. Stay there as long as you like," I said, settling down next to him. *Stay forever.*

Chapter 13

Caleb

I left Teracht's house Sunday evening, feeling exhausted and renewed at the same time. Teracht had edged me for hours on his web. It had been a little disconcerting to be unable to move while my body rode out the pleasure he had given me, but it had also been an oddly strange relief. I couldn't do anything, I couldn't move, I couldn't see anything. There was nothing I could do except lie there, trust Teracht, and accept the pleasure he was giving me. And when my mind had started to drift to things it shouldn't, Teracht was right there with the remote, changing the toy inside of me to distract me back to nothing except the delicious torture. I could tell that he had been having just as much fun as I had by making me writhe, and I had even heard him make a few sounds of pleasure when my body had jerked on his web. My sweet spider was so determined to not be a villain, and yet he was so evil and cruel in the best of ways.

We texted back and forth the next few days. Tuesday, I went to physical therapy, and for the first time since the weather had gotten cold, I did not hide my face with a scarf as I walked into the office. There were a few stares, but no one said anything unkind, and I felt the tiniest bit of the old Caleb return. The Caleb who had a smile for everyone, who was a bit of a flirt, who had just a hint of swagger to him. I felt better than I had in the almost eight months since my life had been turned upside down.

I had a package sent to Teracht's house, with instructions for him not to open it until I came over. Friday evening, I went to Jade Garden by my apartment. I had ordered from them many times, but I had not been in the restaurant in person since before my accident. I had called ahead so my food was ready, and Yan, the elderly Chinese lady, had it at the register for me when I walked in. She did the serving and cashiering while her husband, Hao, whom everyone called Howie, did the cooking. Yan did a double-take as I walked in before she broke into a beaming smile. "Been a long time since I saw you," she said with her accented voice.

"Yeah, I was dealing with a lot," I said as I stopped at the register.

She nodded sagely, looking over my uncovered face and the dangling sleeve of my jacket. "But doing okay now?"

"Better," I replied.

"Good," she said, nodding her head so the light caught the silver strands in her dark hair. "That's a lot of food for one. You have a friend?"

"Boyfriend," I said, realizing that was the first time I had called Teracht that to anyone else.

"You tell him I say he has to take care of you," she said, and I beamed.

"I will. Thank you, Yan."

I pulled my scarf over my face again as I carried the bag of hot Chinese food to Teracht's house. Baby steps to show my face to the world, but it was better than it had been even a month ago.

I grinned excitedly when I saw the box sitting by the couch when Teracht let me in. "Oh good, it did come. I want to try something."

Ter's eyes blinked curiously, and he took the bag with the Chinese food to the kitchen before returning. "What is it?"

I moved over to the box, trying to dig my fingers under the paper tape that held it closed. Ter slid the point of one of his legs across the tape. It split easily. "I love your built-in box cutters," I said, and he giggled.

I reached in, glad to find a plastic handle on the interior box, so I grabbed it and lifted it out from the paper nest, setting it on the ground. Ter stared at it. "What is that?"

"It's a blender," I said. "A good one too. It can blend just about anything."

"Blend?" Ter asked curiously, and I felt a little surge of pride at being able to explain it to him.

"It has a blade inside of it, and you put solid food inside of it. And the blade spins and chops it up. If you let it go long enough, it turns almost any food into a liquid."

Ter inhaled in surprise. "Really?"

I nodded. "I haven't tried it with most foods, but I have an older model of this that I use to make smoothies, and it's great. It's really powerful. You could puree a brick if you wanted to."

Teracht wrinkled his nose. "I am not sure that I would like to drink a brick."

I tried not to snort with laughter. "No, of course not. But that's just how powerful it is."

"You are going to blend solid food?" Teracht asked curiously, and I nodded.

"Yeah. Going to try, at least. If you hate it, I won't be offended, but it might give you some more options."

Teracht smiled hopefully and followed me to the kitchen where I unpackaged the blender and washed it in the sink before setting it up and opening the containers of Chinese food. Fried rice, orange chicken, and, of course, egg rolls. I decided to just start with the fried rice to see if proof of concept even worked. Sure enough, it did. The concoction looked horrific, and it didn't exactly smell as good as it had before I blended it, but watching the delight in Teracht's face as I poured the mixture into a glass was worth it.

"How is it?" I asked after he took a swallow, curious if my little science experiment had been successful.

Ter smacked his lips thoughtfully. "It is… different," he said. "But I think I like it."

I grinned. "We can try other foods too. I'm sure your taste buds aren't used to a lot of things. Wait, do spiders even have taste buds?"

Ter looked thoughtful. "I can taste this food, if that is what you're asking."

I nodded. "What does it taste like?"

"I don't know," Teracht replied, giving my words more consideration than I thought he would. "I have not tasted food like it before."

"But, it's good?" I prompted, and he nodded, giving me a smile that lit up his whole face and made all eight of his dark eyes shine.

"Yes, it's good."

I blended the chicken and the egg rolls for him. Teracht declared that once again, egg rolls tasted nothing like eggs and were very confusing, but he agreed that they were tasty. I watched him savor the orange chicken puree as I ate my own solid version. I was glad that he enjoyed it, though watching my monster boyfriend drink Chinese food from a glass had not been on my relationship bingo card.

Once we were done and had cleaned up, I settled on the couch, and Teracht perched on his web above me. "Caleb, could I make a request of you?" he asked.

"Sure," I said, stretching out my legs a little. "What's up?"

"I... Did you enjoy last weekend?"

"Yeah, I did," I said. "It was a lot of fun. Did *you* enjoy it?"

"Yes, very much," Teracht said, and I watched several of his spider feet fidget.

"But?" I prompted.

Teracht blinked two of his eyes, looking back at me again, cheeks dark. "Do you remember when we were outside, and I mentioned to you that I used to chase prey?"

I nodded. "Yeah, you said that's why you didn't have a pet."

"Yes." Teracht's feet continued to shuffle. He was definitely nervous. I had a feeling in my gut of where this might be going.

"Okay. What's your request?"

Teracht's face grew darker still, and he pressed his hands to his cheeks, as if to hold back the blush. "I..."

"You don't get to come until you tell me what it is," I teased. I think I almost killed him with that comment, as he nearly lost his grip on his web, staring at me through his fingers.

"Would you let me chase you?" he blurted out.

Chapter 14

Teracht

Why, oh why, had I asked him that? He had already given me so much. He trusted in me, let me tie him up and pleasure him, he slept next to me on my web, he bought me a blender and brought Chinese food for me, and I was so ungrateful and asking too much of him. I opened my mouth to tell him to forget it, that it was just a silly thought, but he interrupted me.

"Like, I climb around your web, and you catch me?"

My face was going to burst into flame, I was sure of it. I nodded once, peering at him with several of my eyes through my fingers.

"I mean, with how fast you can move, I'm pretty sure that would last a whole two seconds," Caleb said, glancing around at the webbing that covered my home.

"I wouldn't catch you right away," I mumbled around my hands.

"Oh, so you want to play with your food?" he asked with a small smirk.

If there had been a hole nearby, I would have crawled into it and died. "I'm sorry, that's horrible of me!"

"Babe, I'm joking," Caleb said, and his new nickname for me prompted me to pull my face from my hands to look at him. If he was aware of what he had called me, he wasn't making a big deal out of it. He looked thoughtful before he said, "Sure. As long as you don't injure me, I'll let you chase me."

I gaped at him for a long moment, and then suddenly I launched myself at him, catching him in my arms to give him a kiss. "Oh, thank you, Caleb! That makes me so excited!" He jumped at my sudden movement, and I felt the rush of his heartbeat. I pulled back a little, the blush returning once more. "I'm sorry, I didn't mean to scare you."

He laughed, a sound that I wanted to hear every day. "It really means that much to you?"

"I know that you trust me," I said. "And I want to bring you so much pleasure. I think it would just add more pleasure for me."

He blinked. "Well, I want you to feel pleasure too. So, yeah, we can try it."

"That's not selfish of me?" I asked hopefully.

"What? No, of course not," Caleb said, his voice

surprisingly gentle. "Even if I know you like getting me off and making me feel good, I want you to feel good too. That's how a relationship should work."

He was so understanding. I couldn't have asked for a better boyfriend. His willingness gave me the courage to add, "I did have another idea."

"You and your ideas," he said with a dramatic groan, flopping back against the couch. "If you're going to ask me to wear a fly costume, I might have to draw the line."

I laughed. As cute as Caleb would look in a pair of wings, that wasn't what I had planned. "I was thinking of buying something, but I wanted to ask you first. I promise it's not a fly costume."

"Okay then, what is it?" Caleb said, sitting up again.

I pulled out my phone and pulled up a webpage, holding it out for him to see, hoping he would be too distracted by my phone to see how red my face was. The page showed a strap-on harness, with a variety of dildos that could be attached to it. I had done a rather ridiculous amount of research this week on various harnesses, attachments, and other instruments that could mimic sexual organs. Humans really did love sex and got very creative with it sometimes.

Caleb stared at it for a long moment before he turned his eyes up toward me. "You want to use a strap-on with me?" he asked. I had worried he might be upset, but he sounded curious more than anything.

"It was a thought," I said, pulling the phone back. "But

only if you wanted to."

"I haven't used one before, but I'd be open, if you think that's something you want to try out." He glanced at where my torso connected to the rest of my spider form. "It might take a little creative strapping though."

I laughed, louder than I meant to, probably from nervousness. "I'm not worried about that part. But are you really all right with it? And of course, you can stop at any time if you don't like it."

Caleb sat up on his knees so he could be eye to eye with me. "Yes, I'm all right with it. Maybe just don't go for the biggest dildo option our first time around. Deal?"

"Deal," I said and kissed him firmly.

"And when you're chasing me, don't give me a heart attack either," he said.

"I won't," I said.

He pulled back to look into my eyes. "Will you do something for me too?"

I nodded. "Yes, of course."

He took my hand in his, giving it a squeeze. "After we do this, you go out with me. To a restaurant."

I blinked all eight of my eyes at the unexpected request. "You mean, leave my house?"

"Yes," Caleb said. "I'll be right by your side the entire time. I'll support you, and you support me." He raised his right arm up so I could see the stump. "I want to try going out into the world without... without covering myself up."

It was not an inappropriate request. We were dating, after all, and dates tended to happen outside of a single location. My stomach fluttered nervously. "Is it because you hope people will be too distracted by me to pay attention to you?" I asked, trying to cover the discomfort at the thought of going outside into the world.

Caleb let out a splutter, his cheeks turning red. "No!" he said. "I wouldn't ever want you to feel that way!"

I laughed and leaned in to give him another kiss. "I'm teasing you," I said. Though now that I had said it, I wasn't completely sure I was. People would likely look at me before noticing Caleb, and I was more monstrous by comparison. But he had already done so much for me. This was a step I could take to help him, and he wasn't going to leave me alone. We would face the world together. I took a deep breath and nodded slowly. "Okay. Yes. As long as you are with me."

Caleb held my hand tightly. "If you can take a break on Monday, we could go out for lunch. It's supposed to rain, and it's a weekday, so most places shouldn't be very busy. And we can go to some place we know is monster friendly. You can even choose the location if you want."

"I would like that," I said. Cael would know of a place that would be good to go. Caleb leaned in and pressed his mouth to mine. I reached up to hold his cheeks gently as I returned the kiss. When we both pulled back to breathe, I stared into his eyes, seeing my own midnight ones reflected there. There was another thing I had been thinking about all week besides chasing him and harnesses, and I licked my lips nervously. "Caleb, is it too soon for me to say that I love you?"

Caleb blinked, staring at me for a moment, and my heart stuttered in my chest. Had I said the wrong thing, and now he was going to be upset?

"I... Ter, that's... You do?" His cheeks were bright red.

I nodded slowly. "I think so. I'm not entirely sure, of course. I've never been in love. But I know that I like you a lot, and I want you to be my boyfriend, and I'm happy when you're around me, and you make me feel good, and I want to make you feel good, and maybe that's love, but maybe it's not, and I don't-." I cut myself off. I was overthinking it, and that wasn't helping either of us. "No, I'm sure of it. I love you." Caleb's face was flushed, his skin hot under my touch. "It's all right if you don't. I just want to be honest with you."

He nodded, and I felt tension in my stomach as I waited for him to say something. I didn't expect him to say he loved me back. It probably wasn't even fair of me to put him in that position. He was a human, and he could walk away any time he wanted, and go back to a relatively normal life. My life would never be like that. There would always be pieces of me that would never be 'normal' or 'human,' no matter how much I learned or tried to adapt to this world. I would always be an outsider to some, a threat, a monster.

Caleb exhaled softly, squeezing my hand. "I don't know what to say."

"You don't have to say anything," I said. My chest felt too tight. Had I ruined our relationship by saying words I wasn't supposed to? Did he not feel the same way?

"No, I... Teracht, I care about you, a lot. You've made me feel things that I haven't felt, well, ever. Even before my accident. And the ways you've touched me and talked to me and treated me, it's been... I don't know, it's been so helpful. You're so honest and kind, even when I was a total asshat to you when we first met. And I can't express how much that means to me." Caleb grinned sheepishly. "And now I'm rambling too, but I think what I'm trying to say is, I love you too."

Heat burned behind all eight of my eyes. I couldn't cry, but if I could, I would be right now. "Caleb."

He was in my arms, holding me around the neck as our lips meshed together in a passionate embrace, his hand tangling lightly into my hair, and I mirrored the action in his. We stayed there for a long time, just holding onto one another, letting our warmth mingle and skin touch, before Caleb finally pulled away, giving me a playful poke in the side. "All right, all right, you have a harness to buy. You better get rush shipping on that."

I gave him a bright smile and winked one of my eyes at him. "Yes, sir."

Chapter 15

Caleb

I stayed over Friday night with Teracht, curled up next to him in his web. I woke up Saturday morning to a phone message from the director of one of the local branches of a disability advocacy group; she wanted to know if I was available to meet for coffee on Sunday morning, as she was going to be in Edgewind. I called her back, and we set up a meeting for the next day. Teracht immediately sent me home, saying he would get things prepared for our game Sunday evening.

I needed a haircut. My hair stylist, Lynn, was surprised to hear from me after so long, but she squeezed me in at her house that evening when I offered to bring her a bottle of her favorite fancy wine that she couldn't usually afford. She was a little shocked at my appearance at first, but as soon as

I mentioned that I had a new boyfriend and that he was a monster, she wanted all the details, and we spent the evening chatting like we used to. Apparently, she had been flirting with a couple monsters on the app too and was working on setting up first dates with a few of them. I hoped she'd be as lucky as I had been.

I went through my wardrobe of nicer clothes that I hadn't touched in months. Most of my outfits from before the crash had become impractical overnight. I had resorted to wearing clothes that were easy to pull on and off with one hand without rubbing on my scars, which usually meant they were baggy and not flattering. Finding something that looked nice and that I could get on and off easily took much longer than it should have.

I met with Theresa on Sunday. She was a double amputee who had lost her legs below the knee to a rare form of bone cancer. She worked for National Disability Advocacy, which was created for people who had lost limbs and were adapting to the changes that came with it. They did work both within local communities and nationally to educate people and businesses in how to support individuals dealing with physical or mental disability. I had run across a few groups like this since I had gotten out of the hospital, but my mental state had never been in a place where I felt it was productive to talk to any of them. It was a lot to add on top of the sudden changes I encountered directly after the crash, and I had struggled for a while. I confessed that to her over our lattes.

"That's very understandable and very common," she said as she nibbled at her cranberry-apple muffin. "Our whole system doesn't do the best job at preparing people for those sorts of changes. That's why we're here, to help support people who have questions or needs that are not being addressed, and to make lawmakers aware of what they can do to positively impact those living with impairments."

"I like the idea of having a place I could go to, even if I didn't have a disability, to learn more about how people are affected," I said thoughtfully. "I'm sure my partner would like resources like that too."

"Your partner?" Theresa asked.

I flushed. Not everyone was all right with monsters, I reminded myself. But Theresa was so kind and understanding that I found myself telling her about how I met Teracht, and all of the kindness he had shown me when I was so down on myself and felt like giving up. When she found out my boyfriend was a monster, her hazel eyes lit up. "Oh! It's still being fleshed out, but there's been some talk recently for NDA to potentially offer services for monsters too. Would you be interested in more information about that when I have it?"

"Yeah! That sounds really interesting," I said. "I'm sure Teracht would be interested in hearing about it too. He might even have some ideas."

"We'd love that," Theresa said eagerly. "What does he

currently do?"

I told her, without going into the sexy details, of course, about the webs that Teracht spun for the military and medical research. I explained the comfort I felt on my own damaged skin from Teracht's webs, and she was curious to find out more about the research. We parted with a plan for her to reach out to me later in the week after she had met with the regional office team. I texted Teracht to tell him how my talk with Theresa had gone. He seemed even more excited about it than I was and promised to provide a web sample for me to bring to my next meeting with her.

That evening, my heart was beating so loudly in my chest as I approached Teracht's front door that I almost couldn't hear myself knock on it. Butterflies fluttered in my stomach, battering like they wanted to get out. He had texted me to be ready to start the game as soon as I walked in the door. I had no idea what that would entail, if I would just enter and then immediately get jumped by a giant spider. I hoped that wasn't the case. As eager as I was to try the strap-on toy that he had overnighted, I figured we both would want to stretch the game out at least a little bit. I trusted Teracht, and I knew that even if there were moments where I was afraid, he would not hurt me. The times we had done things together had been amazing, better than any of my previous hookups, and his communication and checking in was reassuring. I trusted him completely and knew that he only wanted me to enjoy it. But I still felt like I was about to encounter a jump scare in a horror movie, knowing it was coming but not sure what to expect.

The door opened, and Teracht smiled at me. "Hello, pet."

"Hi, babe," I said, stepping inside. He had barely closed the door before he grabbed me with several of his spider legs, drawing me in close, and mashing our mouths together in a heated kiss. I groaned, my arms going around his neck. He nosed down my throat, giving it soft nips before he reached the collar of my coat and pulled back to gaze at me. "Undress. Now."

The simple command went straight to my dick. "Yes, sir," I said, trying to get out of my jacket so quickly I nearly got tangled in it. I toed off my boots and slid off my socks, then quickly shucked off my shirt, pants, and underwear into a heap on the floor, until I was naked in front of him. Teracht eyed me up and down like he was assessing a delicious steak dinner. "Mm. Get on your knees and bend down."

I blinked, not expecting that command, but I quickly lowered myself to my knees, then down onto my forearms. Teracht stepped over me, his abdomen brushing my back, which sent a shiver through me. He reached down and parted my ass cheeks before one lubed, gloved finger suddenly pushed inside me with no hesitation. I couldn't stop a sudden sound of surprise, and Teracht quickly glanced over at me. "All right?"

"Yeah. I mean, yes, sir," I said. I wasn't sure what he was doing, but the fact that he had been waiting for me, all prepped for this, made me chuckle to myself. My eager little spider dom. His finger stretched me for a moment before he pulled it out, and then something cold and slick pushed against my entrance. I gasped, muscles clenching before relaxing, and I felt the cold of the stainless steel butt plug stretch me wide before sinking into my heat and securing itself there. "Fuck," I groaned softly.

Teracht gave my left ass cheek a nip. "Is that all right, pet?"

"Yes, sir," I said, my hips giving a push back towards his mouth.

"Good. I am going to give you sweet pleasure while I chase you," Teracht replied, giving the end of the plug a nudge with his finger. The thing suddenly began to buzz, and I jumped, the sensation going straight to my groin.

"Fuck... Isn't that... going to give you an advantage over me?" I asked. It was on the lowest setting, and I was already getting distracted.

"Of course. But I have all of the advantages anyway. And I want you to be ready for me when I catch you."

No worries about that. Teracht could have taken me right there in the entryway, and I would have welcomed it. I lifted my head to look around and realized that the lights had been dimmed much lower than usual, the dying sunlight through the windows the brightest bit of light in the house. Teracht's webs still were strung over the entire house, but something about them looked different. I realized that he had probably discarded all of them and made a completely new web for this.

"Now, pet," Teracht purred, leaning down over me and covering me with his large body, his mouth pressed to my ear, making me shiver. "You get two minutes to run before I chase you. I rebuilt all of my webbing so you shouldn't stick to it easily. You can go anywhere you want, climb any of it." The tip of his tongue brushed my ear, making me shiver. "But when I catch you, and I will, I'm going to pleasure you until you beg for mercy." Fuck, that was hot. I almost didn't want to run. I could already feel sweat breaking out on my skin. Teracht's tongue brushed the back of my neck, licking up a droplet of sweat there. "You can use your safe word at any time if you want to. What is it?"

"Gatorade," I whispered obediently, and he gave me several kisses down my spine in reward.

"Good. Do you have any questions?"

"No, sir," I said, pressing up a little so I could feel more of his abdomen against my back. He laughed and pulled away.

"You will get plenty of that later, pet. For now, I suggest you run." He gave my right shoulder a nip, then gave my left ass cheek a smack with his palm.

I yelped and got to my feet, the plug shifting inside of me a little as I stood. Despite knowing this was all in good fun, my body still felt on high alert, like I was already being stalked by an unseen entity. I hurried inside the living room, glad to see that Teracht had added a few makeshift web ladders for me to climb. I grabbed one with my hand and began to pull myself up it. It was still sticky, but I was able to pull my hand away with ease if I tried. I took half a second to marvel at how incredible his webs were before I focused on climbing onto the mass of webbing. I already knew he was going to have no trouble catching me, but I wasn't about to make it easy for him either. I ran across the webs; it was woven close enough together that my foot would not slip through anywhere. It felt like running on a trampoline. My little spider had been busy! I grabbed another piece to pull myself up higher. I hadn't exactly been lazy since my accident, but I was definitely not the gym rat I had once been. My muscles were already protesting. I was going to feel this workout for days.

I had no idea how much time had passed, but I figured my two minutes had to be almost up. I found a small, darker alcove under the overhang from his second-floor hallway and tucked myself into it, trying to quiet my breathing that suddenly sounded loud as fuck in the stillness.

I hadn't realized how quiet Teracht's house was until I was the only thing in it making noise. I could hear the faint buzz and hum of the refrigerators and other electronics, and the muted vibration of the plug inside of me, but otherwise, it was as if I were alone in the house. I was already slightly creeped out by that. Imagining I was entering a dark cave or woods covered in giant spider webs, knowing that I was crunchy and tasted good, would have been an absolute nightmare. But knowing that Teracht wasn't going to hurt me, and the pleasant buzz coming from the plug inside me was keeping me calm. Well, calmer.

The plug's pitch suddenly changed, the vibrations getting more intense, and I sucked in a breath, clapping my right forearm to my mouth to stifle a moan as the sensation went through me, making my cock twitch. I knew Teracht could see me from wherever he was and was probably laughing to himself at how much he was teasing me. I tried not to shift in my position, my heart pounding as my ass pulsed around the plug.

Wherever Teracht was, he was completely silent, which creeped me out. I wasn't even 'prey' in the most literal sense right now, and I was still slightly terrified. I wondered if he could smell the fear and anxiety on my skin. Maybe it turned him on. I hadn't ever considered fear to cause a sexual response, but damn, I was understanding it now. Knowing that it wasn't a matter of *if* he would catch me, but *when*, knowing that he was going to pleasure me, probably edge me like he had the last weekend, until I begged him for mercy, was fucking with my head in the best ways. I wanted to get caught, but I also wanted to give him a run for his money and hopefully give him the pleasure of the chase that he had been missing.

A dark shadow passed over my hiding area, and I froze.

I knew it was him. He knew exactly where I was, but he continued past my hiding spot, higher up onto the web. I gave it a minute, but he didn't come back. The playful bastard wanted me to run. I cautiously crawled from my corner, peering out. I couldn't see him in the tangle of webbing, but I suspected he was somewhere above me. That wasn't creepy or anything. I scrambled to my feet and made a dash across the webs toward a little tunnel-like structure. I had almost made it when the plug changed vibrations again, and I slipped and landed on my side, closing my eyes for a moment as the pleasure spiked through me. I was momentarily paralyzed between getting up and running, or just lying there and letting the pleasure take over. But when no giant spider swooped down on my fallen form, I got to my feet and dove into the tunnel.

There wasn't much light to see by in here, but I could see the other end a short distance away and could see that he was not lurking in the tunnel waiting for me. It was tall enough that we both could have fit, but it would have been a tight squeeze. I army-crawled on my belly through the webbing, the fibers of it ruffling the fine hairs on my body and sensitizing each one. Every movement felt heightened even more, as if his spider feet were caressing my skin. I reached the end of the tunnel, peering cautiously out. I didn't see anything, and nothing moved. I slid out of the tunnel, getting carefully to my feet. The high-pitched hum of the plug inside me sounded almost deafening loud. There was no hiding my location with that. Not that I would have been able to hide from Teracht anyway. My sweet little pleasure dom was still an apex predator, no matter how cute he seemed.

I continued to move around the webs, climbing onto higher or lower levels, my body protesting. I needed to get back into working out. Every once in a while, a shadow would move, and my heart would nearly leap out of my chest as I would turn, only to find nothing. He was absolutely toying with me, but he must have been enjoying himself if he was letting it continue. I had no idea how long it had been since we started. In the silence, everything seemed like an eternity. The plug suddenly changed rhythm twice in rapid succession, and my cock gave a responding twitch as I leaned against one of the webbed walls to steady myself. Sadistic jerk. He was driving me absolutely crazy, and he knew it. He also knew that I loved it, if my cock dripping between my legs was any indication.

Something dark moved above me, and I turned and ran the opposite direction, not sure where I was going but feeling the animalistic instinct to get away. Something caught around my foot, and I tripped, yelping as I pitched over the edge of one of the webs. But it was a thick strand of Teracht's silk, and I found myself dangling upside down by my ankle, the ground still a foot or two beneath me. My hair fell into my face, and I shoved it and some sweat out of my eyes as I rotated in the air like a piece of meat on a spit. I squirmed, trying to engage my abs to keep myself from flopping gracelessly around.

And then he was looming over me in the dimness, grabbing the strands that currently held me from hitting the ground. His legs went around me to support me as he lifted me back onto the web I had fallen off of, surprisingly gentle considering the situation. Then he pressed me down face-first onto the web. He ran his tongue up the back of my ear, like he was tasting me, and I shivered, struggling under him, even as heat spiked in my veins.

Teracht suddenly grabbed the base of the plug that was still buzzing inside of me and pulled it from my body with an obscene pop. I let out a groan at the loss of stimulation, then froze when I felt something else push at my pulsing entrance. I was able to turn my head just enough to see that Teracht did indeed have the strap-on harness with one of the dildos attached to it. The purple silicone phallus gleamed slick with lube already, and I barely had a moment to brace for it before Teracht grabbed my hips and shoved the first inch inside of me. The stretch made me gasp, my fingers gripping the web underneath me, but the sudden ache quickly faded as he settled on top of me, grinding down against me to push it further into me. I whined, squirming under him, torn between the urge to fight back and the urge to lie still and accept my inevitable fucking.

"No more fight in you, pet?" he said, his voice teasing. Oh, so he did want me to resist. I grinned to myself and grabbed at the webs in front of me with my fingers, trying to pull myself free from under him. I did move, a very tiny amount, but he simply grabbed me and pulled me back under him like I weighed nothing, causing the strap-on to shift inside of me. I whimpered as pleasure pulsed through me before I suddenly shoved upward against him. Obviously, he had not been expecting that, because he actually fell back a few steps. I had surprised myself by suddenly being free as well, and I think he took more time to recover than he actually needed, giving me a chance to scramble to my feet and start to run, my heart in my throat.

I didn't make it far. He launched himself at me and caught me in his arms, and we rolled several feet on the webbing, me clutched to his abdomen protectively, but also so I was not able to get free. As soon as we stopped, he pinned me onto my back, giving me a deliciously wicked grin. His spider feet came up, and my left hand and wrist and my right forearm were suddenly pinned above my head, tied in place with his silk. He leaned down and pressed his mouth to mine hungrily. His primal kiss sent heat surging inside of me, and I bucked up against him eagerly.

The next moment, he lifted my right knee almost to my chest and lashed several strands of silk around the back of my thigh, which he connected to the webbing underneath me. He repeated the movement with my left leg, almost faster than I could process, but I did realize that I was bent double, stretched obscenely wide for him as he loomed over me. He grinned and positioned the dildo at my entrance again, and then slid inside me in one long, smooth stroke.

The cry of pleasure that escaped my lips was the only part of me that was going anywhere as he pinned me to the web with his torso, taking a moment to find his rhythm with the unfamiliar movement of his hips against mine. Several of his eyes gave me a quick once-over, asking silently if I was all right, and I nodded in return, my back arching as he thrust deep inside of me. Teracht purred and ran his tongue up my neck, grinding his hips into me, and I let out a strangled yowl of pleasure. He seemed delighted by that reaction and did it again. My body pulsed and spasmed under him as he ground against me, and I knew I wasn't going to last long under him. "Please," I moaned as his hips thrust the strap-on deep inside of me. "Please, let me come."

"Come for me, pet," he whispered into my ear, slamming his hips into me again as his hand wrapped around my cock and stroked. It only took a few more thrusts before I did, covering my own stomach and his with my release. But the pounding into my ass didn't stop as I rode out the waves of pleasure. Teracht continued to thrust into me, harder and faster, his hand stroking my over-sensitized length, my come lubricating the whole thing in a sticky mess. It felt so good that it almost hurt, and I couldn't hold back a scream of pained pleasure, writhing and jerking under him, my body trapped beneath him as he used me. I think I cursed, sounds coming out of my mouth, but I had no idea what they were.

I only knew Teracht, his body pinning mine as he slammed harder still into me, his hand stroking my still-hard cock. My senses were in overdrive, every touch like lightning on my skin, every brush like being stung and kissed at the same time.

He thrust deep inside of me as he kissed me, and I cried out against his mouth, my lips hungry on his as I whimpered and struggled, wanting more of his touch but less of it at the same time. He ground hard against me, and my vision went white for a minute as I screamed into his mouth. My cock lurched as another orgasm rocked me, wringing a small amount of come out of me and over his hand. His tongue thrust deep into my mouth and down my throat, claiming me, and my own tongue fought his for dominance. He grabbed my hair with his free hand, yanking my head back, and he bit down on the scarred skin where my neck and shoulder connected. I knew he hadn't broken the skin with his flat teeth, but the sweet agony flooded my body, and I felt the world fall out from under me until there was nothing but pleasure from his slender embrace.

When I came to, I was on the couch, my silk bindings gone, a blanket over me, and a pillow under my head. Teracht held a straw to my lips, and I sipped at the beverage without registering what it was. His pointed fingers stroked through my hair gently. "Rest, Caleb." I didn't need to be told twice. I think I was asleep before my eyes were even fully closed again.

I must have slept hard, because it was morning, sunlight coming in through the windows, when I opened my eyes. My whole body hurt, but not in the way that it had when I had woken up in the hospital after my accident. This was a good hurt, one that reminded me of the thrill of being chased, caught, and pounded into until I screamed. I felt sticky, but I could tell Teracht had at least tried to clean me up a little before putting me to bed on the couch. I sat up, scrubbing at my eyes, wincing a little at the ache inside of me.

"Good morning," Teracht said, appearing at my side with a bottle of juice with a straw, holding it out to me.

"Good morning," I said. My voice was a little rough, like I had been screaming at a rock concert.

"Are you all right?" he asked, settling next to me as I took the beverage and swallowed several sips gratefully. "I worried I might have overdone it."

"No, I'm just fine," I said, giving him a grin, and he immediately relaxed a little. "God, that was... scary and fun."

"Did you like it?" Teracht asked hopefully.

I nodded, stretching my arms up. "Yeah. I need to exercise more before I do anything else like that though. Ouch."

Teracht giggled, leaning in to kiss me. "You were so beautiful."

I blushed a little. "Thank you. Did you have fun?"

He nodded eagerly, then ducked his head. "So much fun."

"We can do it again sometime," I offered, and he beamed in delight.

"Really?"

"Yes, really," I said. I pushed the blanket off of myself, finding I was still naked. I got my feet under me, then winced as I put my weight into standing. "Fuck. Might need to wait a little while though, you really did a number on me."

"I'm sorry," Teracht said, reaching out to help steady me.

I leaned in and kissed him. "It was amazing, don't you dare apologize for it. We both had fun, and no damage done."

Teracht nodded and kissed me back. "I have to start spinning for work. Are we still going to go out for lunch today?"

"Do you still want to?" I asked. If he had changed his mind, I wouldn't push him.

He looked slightly nervous, but he nodded. "Yes. As long as you are with me."

"Every step of the way," I promised.

Chapter 16

Teracht

CALEB SHOWERED, AND THEN he sat on the couch, and we chatted as I spun my webs that would be picked up by the military at the end of the day. I had already spun extra while Caleb was sleeping to ensure I did not miss my usual quota when we went out for our lunch date. I was more than a little nervous. I would be going outside, going to somewhere other than the military base for the first time since I had entered the human world. But I was doing it with the most amazing, beautiful human by my side.

"Ready?" Caleb asked, slipping his hand into mine.

I exhaled and squeezed his fingers back. "I think so."

"We can do this," he replied firmly.

I nodded and reached for the lock. The click of it echoed in the silence between us. I turned the door handle and pulled the front door open. Caleb lifted my hand to his lips to give it a soft kiss before he took a step outside, drawing me out after him.

I stepped onto the porch steps, and Caleb's hand left mine as he moved behind me to close and lock the front door, pocketing the key, before he took my hand. "All right so far?"

"Yes," I said softly, glancing around. There weren't that many people out, it being a weekday and rather gloomy outside, the heavy clouds threatening rain. Caleb took a step off the porch, and I followed after him. My feet touched the concrete path leading to my front gate, and I made a face. I much preferred the smoothness of walls and the softness of my webs, and the sidewalk was probably covered in dirt and grime, but I was not going to let Caleb down.

Caleb motioned to the closed gate. "You want to do the honors?"

Considering I was the one with the free hand, I nodded, reaching out to unlatch it. It squeaked a little as it swung, inviting us through. I lifted my chin, gave Caleb a hopeful smile, and slid my bulky body out through the gate and onto the public sidewalk. And then Caleb was next to me, holding my hand reassuringly as he gave the gate a pull with his foot to mostly close it.

A drop of water landed on my head, and I looked up in surprise. The rain was starting. Caleb glanced up too. "Hey, great timing, right? Come on. Let's go get something to eat."

It wasn't the easiest to see with the gloom and the rain

starting to fall, but that didn't stop my eight eyes from roaming around. The last time I had been outside my own front gate was when I went to the military base for my naturalization classes, and that had been nearly a year ago. The world looked so different seeing it with my own eyes rather than through a window or a TV screen. The air had a strange smell to it too, a sort of damp, musty odor that, while not pleasant, was different than what I was used to. The soft drops of water falling onto my head and body was a little disconcerting, since rain in the monster world could potentially be harmful, but here, it was just cold. Caleb's hair was damp and clinging to his forehead, and I reached up to brush it lightly away with a fingertip. He glanced over at me. He looked strangely happy, and the sight made my heart dance a little in my chest. He was so beautiful, and he was all mine, by my side, supporting me, as I was supporting him.

A few people were waiting at the bus stop as we passed, shivering in jackets and under umbrellas. A few looked over at us and stared in surprise. I felt the weight of their eyes like a crushing boulder on top of me, and my feet shuffled for just a moment. Caleb squeezed my hand firmly. "Come on, babe," he said, his voice low for only me to hear. "You're doing great."

We passed the group, and one of them turned to mutter something to her companion that neither of us were able to hear. But Caleb only drew me on, lifting his chin higher. I was starting to see the confidence he had once exuded in his photos. The sort of easy grace, the don't-give-a-fuck attitude, the look that said you would be lucky to have me. And I was lucky enough to have him. He was mine, all mine. My boyfriend was the best boyfriend.

The coffee shop was only another few blocks away, but both of us were nearly soaked through when we reached Brewed For You. The windows glowed with a soft, yellow light, and I was glad to see that, while there were a few patrons inside, not all of whom were human either, the space was not crowded.

The college-age girl behind the counter had blond hair with pink and blue streaks in it. I wanted to touch them, but I figured that might not be acceptable without consent. Maybe Caleb would dye his hair fun colors for me if I asked. She stared at me for a moment before she gave me a smile that she also turned on Caleb. "Hi, what can I get you two?"

I realized that I had never been to a place like this before and had absolutely no idea what to order or even where to look to find the information that would be helpful. I turned to Caleb, giving him a shy smile. "Will you pick something for me?"

Caleb gazed back at me, then nodded and gave my hand a squeeze before he turned back to the girl at the register, ordering a salad for himself and several different beverages for me, none of which I knew, but all of which sounded like they would be delicious. He reached for his wallet in his jeans, but I stole it with several of my feet and put it back as my hand slid into his jacket pocket to retrieve my phone with the attached card slot. "I got it," Caleb protested, but I just shook my head while the girl at the register watched us with amusement.

I held out the card to her, and she took it, not seeming too concerned with how close our fingers were in the exchange. That was a little strange, to not feel fear from someone besides Caleb, but it was nice. I was glad she did not seem afraid of me. She handed me back my card and a slip of paper. Caleb gave me a tug over to an unoccupied table. He removed one of the two chairs there and replaced it with a stool from nearby, obviously intended for monstrous patrons who could not fit in regular chairs. Not everywhere would be so accommodating, I knew, but for my first outing into the 'real world,' I was grateful. I settled onto the stool with not very much grace, and Caleb looked like he was trying not to laugh at me as he settled into his own chair.

I took his hand across the table once we were seated, and he squeezed it lightly. "Are you doing all right?"

I nodded. There was a lot to take in with the bright lights, all the colors and smells and sounds, and my eight eyes were constantly moving everywhere to watch everything. "Yes. It is a little overwhelming."

Caleb nodded. "I understand that. I promise we can go home after we eat."

I felt warmth course through me at his words. *Go home.* Did Caleb consider my home his too? We hadn't been seeing each other very long, but my house felt empty now when he was not there. I looked forward to the days he came over, and I missed him when he wasn't there. Both of us had been alone for so long, and I didn't want to be without him.

"Will you move in with me?" I blurted out before quickly clapping my hand over my mouth.

Caleb stared at me in surprise. "Move in with you?"

I nodded, slowly pulling my hand away. "Yes. I mean... I would have to confirm it with the military base, and I'm sure there would be paperwork and probably some interviews and clearances and stuff like that. But I like having you around. I miss you when you're not with me."

Caleb hadn't blinked yet, which was rather unsettling. Was that how he felt when I didn't blink for a long time too? "As what?"

"What?" I asked.

"As your roommate? Your friend? Your boyfriend?"

I shook my head, clasping his hand in both of my own. "As my lover. My partner. The most important thing in my life."

"Um..." Caleb said slowly. "I... Ter, are you sure? That's a big step for you. For both of us."

I nodded. "I know. I would not have asked you if I didn't mean it. But if you don't want to, I understand." He might not feel the same way; he might want his privacy, and I would respect that, even if it hurt.

Caleb smiled, and it was brighter than sunshine. "Fuck, Ter. You really want me there, all the time?"

I nodded, giving his hand a squeeze. "I do. I love you. And I want to be able to tell you that in person. I want to watch movies with you, and go to restaurants, and see the mummies. But it might be a while before I'm ready for that last one."

Caleb's blue eyes seemed to fill with tears for a moment before he blinked, and they were gone again. "We can do all of those things together, babe. You talk to the military and make sure it's all right. My lease is up at the end of July. If you get permission, I'll move in with you. If you'll have me."

"Every day!" I said exuberantly, and Caleb blushed, glancing around at the people by us. Luckily, if anyone heard my outburst, they weren't obviously listening in. "I want you with me forever, Caleb. There's no one in this whole world I'd rather be with than you."

Caleb chuckled. "Okay there, Disney princess, need I remind you that I'm one of the only people you've ever even met."

I wasn't entirely sure what he meant by that, but I understood one thing. "If I'm a princess, that makes you my handsome prince."

Caleb gave my hand a squeeze before someone at the counter called a number, and he got up, waving at me to stay put when I started to move. He headed over to the counter, scooping up the tray with his hand and balancing it carefully with his right forearm as he made his way back to the table. He set the tray down, then leaned in to give me a soft kiss.

"I thought the prince was supposed to save the princess, not the other way around." He settled into his chair across from me again.

"We saved each other. Cause that's what true love is. Isn't it?" I asked.

"You watch way too many romance movies," Caleb said as he placed my beverages in front of me in a straight line. "But yeah, I guess that could be true love."

I beamed. "Well, I love you, Caleb Webster."

"And I love you, Teracht Webster."

I blinked in surprise, feeling warmth rush through me. "Do I get to take your name?"

"If you want to. I mean, it's kind of perfect for you, isn't it?" Caleb asked.

"It is," I agreed. "Perfect. Just like you."

Epilogue

Caleb

I MET WITH THERESA a few days after Teracht and I went to
Brewed For You. "I have a proposal for you," she said as we
ate lunch in a corner booth at a diner. "We've recently had
a few monsters reach out to us. They have injuries or have
been in accidents here and are dealing with many of the same
issues humans are when trying to find care and support. But
there's so little known about monsters that it's hard to know
how to go about helping them and offering resources. A lot
of them are just looking for someone to listen. Would you
be interested in being that person? A sort of first point of
contact?"

"As an actual job?" I asked, unable to keep the surprise out
of my tone.

She nodded. "Yes. Paid and benefits and everything."

The idea that I could help other monsters like Teracht who were maybe alone here in the human world was an interesting position, one I had not ever considered might be needed. But with my own background and my monster boyfriend, as well as his military connections, it sounded like a job that had the potential to grow and really do some good for those who needed it. "I'd definitely be interested in talking to you about it further."

Within two weeks, I was onboarded as the first Monster Community Liaison for National Disability Advocacy. Teracht was so excited that he ordered an ice cream cake for us to celebrate, which we happily ate together, though he gave me his cookie crust. We called my parents and FaceTimed with them to tell them about my new job and so they could meet my boyfriend. I had been a little concerned how they would feel about my dating a monster, and if my mom would be creeped out, as she had never been a fan of spiders. But our video chat went well, and my mom texted me later to tell me how sweet Teracht was and how pretty all of his eyes were. I had to agree with her there.

I began to work from home in my new position while Teracht and I hung out together on weekends. He had been right, there were a lot of interviews and paperwork with the military in the approval process to allow me to move into his government-appointed house. But in the end, I was cleared. My parents decided to come visit at the beginning of July to help me pack up and move out of my apartment and so they could meet Teracht in person. "I will make some of those peanut butter cookies you like," my mom gushed when we were arranging details.

"Well, um, Teracht can only eat things that are liquid, but I'll enjoy them," I said. It made me sad that Teracht might not be able to eat something my mom made that I loved so much.

"Hmm." My mom was quiet for a minute before she spoke up again. "I'll crumble them up and put them into vanilla ice cream for him. Would that work?"

My heart soared that my mom was willing to accommodate Teracht's dietary needs, and my little spider did a bit of a happy dance when I told him my mom's suggestion. My dad and Teracht hit it off surprisingly well as they moved boxes from the moving truck into Teracht's house, discussing their love of James Bond movies and MythBusters. By the end of the day, my dad had already promised to take Teracht to see a baseball game whenever we came to visit them. I thought it might be a while before Teracht was up to traveling away from Edgewind, but it was a great goal to work toward.

I took one of the upstairs bedrooms, moving my bed into it, though I suspected I would be sleeping on Teracht's web a lot. It really was super comfortable and helped my burn scars to ache less. The other bedroom became my office, and Teracht left me alone when I had the door closed and was working. I worried that having someone else in the house constantly would throw him off or annoy him, but he seemed as content as ever, watching TV while he spun his webs. He even got into audiobooks, and I came downstairs more than once to find him with his headphones on, utterly absorbed in a story as his spinnerets and feet moved in perfect synchrony.

The first anniversary of my accident came soon after I moved in. I wasn't sure how I was going to feel about it, and it admittedly was hard to get out of bed that day. But Teracht held me close and ordered us Chinese food, and I curled up cocooned in his web for an afternoon nap. My life had changed so drastically, and not all of it had been good. I was still having to adapt in my current circumstances, and I often was dealing with varying levels of pain from my injuries on a daily basis. But I was alive, I had a new job, my parents loved me, and I had the most amazing boyfriend a guy could ask for. I could be doing a lot worse.

"Do you want to go out and see the new Marvel movie tonight?" Teracht asked as we stood at the kitchen counter having an afternoon snack.

I blinked. "Like, go out to a movie theater?"

Teracht nodded. "Cael told me the new monster-friendly movie place just opened last week."

"And you're okay going out?" I asked, making sure to keep it light.

Teracht nodded slowly. "Yes. But, if we can maybe sit in the back row?" he asked hopefully.

Going at all was a big step, let alone him being the one to bring it up. "You bet, babe. We can sit anywhere you'd like."

Teracht sudden tossed a length of webbing around my waist and gave it a yank, sending me sliding across the hardwood floor in my socks, right into his arms. He kissed me firmly. "I love you, Caleb."

I held him tightly, his legs going around me to hold me close to his warm chest. "I love you, Ter, and I'm so proud of you."

Teracht beamed, all eight of his eyes blinking. "You are?"

"Yeah! And so happy I get to be a part of your journey."

Teracht's fingers stroked lovingly through my hair. "*Our* journey, pet," he corrected. "We're doing this together."

I grinned and gave him another kiss on his perfect lips. "Yes, sir."

Acknowledgements

A HUGE SHOUT OUT and thank you to Kristína Lucien, one of my wonderful fans, who gave me many resources and advice on how to approach Caleb's life-altering accident respectfully and responsibly. Some resources she provided that I found very useful were www.livingwithamplitude.com and www.changingfaces.org.uk.

Thank you to all of my beta readers, who fell in love with my cinnamon roll spider and helped me to develop the romantic part of my romance story. An author is only as good as the people who support them, and you are an amazing bunch!

To any of my readers who are dealing with physical or mental health issues, you are not alone. Take care of yourselves, and know that I love you.

About the Author

Kit Barrie (she/her) was raised by pirates in a traveling carnival where she learned how to fly and to weave fantasy into reality. She identifies as chaotic bisexual, with good intentions and questionable methods. She lives in an utterly unfantastical state in the Midwestern United States with her very supportive spouse (VSS) and at least 4 food goblins who might just be cats gobblin' food.

Please visit www.kitbarrie.com or scan the QR code below for more information on Kit and her other available titles.

Additional Titles by Kit Barrie

<u>The Queerly Classic Collection</u>
The Prince on the Lake: A Queer YA Fairy Tale
Midnight Companion: An MM Retelling of The Legend of Sleepy Hollow
X Marks the Spot: A Gay Retelling of Treasure Island

<u>The Hanenea'a Chronicles</u>
The Goblin Twins
A Study in Scholar
The Gift

<u>Standalones</u>

Where the Sky Meets the Sea: An MM Mer Steampunk
Romance

Spinning Out of Control: An MM Monster Romance
(Part of the Monster Match series)

Please consider leaving a review on Amazon, Goodreads, or
other book review site. Reviews are extremely important for
independent authors and are always appreciated.